Holocaust in the Homeland

Black Wall Street's Last Days

Corinda Pitts Marsh

DEDICATION

This story is dedicated to the men, women, and children of Greenwood and in particular to Dr. A.C. Jackson who sought only to do good for his fellow man.

Yours Fraternally,
Dr. A. C. Jackson,
Consulting Physician & Surgeon
Chronic diseases and diseases of Women a Specialty.
Calls made in the country.   Phone 2573   In office at Night.
Corner Greenwood and Archer   Tulsa, Okla.

CONTENTS

Though they fought the sacrificial
Fight, with banners flying high,
Yet the thing of more importance
Is the way they fought—and why!

A. J. Smitherman

ACKNOWLEDGMENTS

I wish to express my appreciation to the Tulsa Reparations Committee, which can be accessed at www.tulsareparations.org. Without their carefully prepared report, this story could not exist. The majority of the material here comes directly from their research. They spent many hours of conscientious research compiling the facts and interviewing survivors. Their report includes material hidden for decades and provides a window to view one of the greatest tragedies of American history. Their dedication to the task is a worthy tribute to a town that suffered so much.

I also wish to thank the Greenwood Cultural Center for their assistance and guidance in preparing this story. All photos and maps included are the property of the Cultural Center and are published here with their gracious permission. Special thanks to Mechelle Brown for her tireless assistance and enthusiasm for this project. The Cultural Center can be accessed at www.greenwoodculturalcenter.com.

.

Cover Image

Geoffrey Adam Brown

Photography by Hudson Guilaran

CHAPTER 1

I HAVE A STORY TO TELL

"Niggers with money," that's what the *Exchange Bureau Bulletin* in Tulsa listed as the cause of the riot that destroyed a town, burned it to the ground, killed possibly 300 people, and left 10,000 homeless. The *Bulletin* was wrong on every level, but their comment sheds light on the real causes: envy, racism, lack of education and understanding, and journalism gone amok. The journalists who wrote those words and the newspapers that published them were a major factor in the events of Memorial Day, 1921, in Tulsa, Oklahoma. The *Bulletin*, however, was not the only or even the most significant guilty party. Other journalists in Tulsa fueled the fire. I'm ashamed to admit I was one of them. I never intended to harm anyone and neither did most of my colleagues, but together we became an animal smelling blood in the water. Good journalists always smell the blood in the water before anyone knows it's there, but they are not supposed to draw the blood. They were a significant link in a chain of events that turned into a holocaust in the homeland. Those journalists forgot that while hype sells, truth protects. If truth had prevailed, none of this would have happened, but that would have hurt newspaper sales.

Unfortunately, stirring the pot in Tulsa was relatively easy. A string of seemingly non-related incidents and a divided town with vast differences in relative wealth and culture created journalistic fodder ripe for disaster. The media boiled the kettle until it spilled over into an unfathomable situation. Add post-Civil War racial tension and disaster was inevitable.

Tulsa had exploded from a small pioneer town into a throng of 100,000 people, and the inevitable crime wave followed. Citizens on both sides of the tracks wanted solutions, but none were forthcoming. Prohibition became the law of the land in 1920. Bootleggers and night clubs satisfied the desire for liquor with illegal hooch or moonshine. When the drunken party goers looked for a woman, someone was always there to satisfy that need. Crime built on crime. Heroin and other hard drugs were readily available. Where there is a market, someone will take advantage of it, and when there is a desire for such vices, some will do anything to procure them. It isn't a new scenario, but it is a deadly one. Human nature wants to blame someone for problems, and humans prefer to place blame whenever possible on ones we perceive as enemies, particularly if we don't know them or we envy them.

In 1921 Greenwood was a section of Tulsa occupied exclusively by African Americans. Greenwood residents traded among themselves. Many had become quite wealthy, but most were simply hard-working men and women, who lived modestly and quietly among others like themselves. The only thing most white Tulsans knew about Greenwood residents was that many of them were wealthy, far more so than most white Tulsans. They never stopped to consider that wealth and good fortune tend to follow hard work and keen insight. So it was in Greenwood.

O. W. Gurley had seized opportunity and established an environment where American capitalism was allowed to flourish. Small men watching this unfold wanted their share of the wealth. On Memorial Day, 1921, some of them took what they perceived to be their share and burned the rest to the ground, a total of 42 blocks of destruction. The following account is an old man's recollection of that fateful holiday turned holocaust and the events that led up to it.

It's been nearly 40 years since I laid eyes on Dick Rowland, but I still wake up in a cold sweat and see his terrified face with those huge round eyes and long eyelashes. The terror keeps me from sleeping.

I kept in touch with Sarah Page for many years as well. We kept in touch maybe because I was her link to Dick in some odd way. She never saw him again after he left Tulsa, but neither did she forget him. She was as helpless as the rest of us once it began, but she never caved in to the demands of the mob. She and Dick were both orphans and really had no one to lean on, but both of them survived the storm, maybe not intact, but they did survive. She was 17 that day. He was 19. They aged a lifetime in 48 hours. I'm still not sure what Rowland was to her, but my gut tells me he was more than "the shoe shine boy." Some say they were "courting," but no one really knows. She says he tripped and fell as he stepped into her elevator on Memorial Day, but a friend told me she cried every night for weeks after that.

Most of us cried in those days, but more Tulsans than I want to believe strutted around and boasted of winning the war. Their perceived victory brought another plague to Tulsa that ruled for decades before reason brought them to ruin or at least forced them into the shadows. That plague walked on two feet and wore a white hood.

Covering the massive growth of Tulsa into a bustling modern town of 100,000 residents, some grand—some not so grand, was quite a lark for a young journalist from the East, but the lark ended abruptly, and I put my pencil down after covering those dark days in Tulsa. I didn't pick it up again until now. I walked away from the rubble and my job at the paper and earned a living on a cattle ranch in Montana until age and arthritis forced me off the range. Shoveling manure seemed far more palatable than stirring human garbage and feeding it to the masses. No one in Montana knew where I came from or that I had been a part of one of the saddest days of this country's history. I was grateful for that. Now the time has come to put the pieces together and try to tell the story that was swept under the rug and kept there for more than half a century. The story was kept so quiet that children born in Tulsa for several decades after were totally unaware that it ever occurred. Even the white population, who were proud of their feat when conversing with their peers, knew not to disclose the facts to the world. Those who were genuinely ashamed would never have dared tell what they knew. Fortunately, some of them talked to me. I became one of them. I held their stories next to my heart until today. Time has dimmed my eyes, but the vision of that day and the people who were a part of it live in a perpetual spotlight in my mind. Most of them have passed away into oblivion, but not in my mind.

Oklahoma was booming, Tulsa in particular. With the influx of oil drilling and exploration after the discovery of the Glenn Pool field in 1905, Tulsa was dubbed the "Oil capital of the world." People flooded in like a human tsunami. They brought with them the dreams, hopes, and vices of human kind. They were a varied throng, and each one of them was there for a reason. Justice was most often the vigilante kind. They took care of crime in the same manner their grandfathers had taken care of cattle rustlers, with a rope and an oak tree or with a whip in some hidden cove or shack.

By 1920, more than 400 different oil and gas companies

called Tulsa home. The city had four different railroad lines, a magnificent new 3,500 seat convention center and auditorium, new schools and city parks, two daily newspapers for the white residents and one for the Greenwood community, seven banks, 200 practicing attorneys, and 150 doctors. More than 10,000 phones were in service and residents had access to modern conveniences such as indoor plumbing and electricity, which much of the country lacked. They even had electric trolleys for transportation. Many of the homes were palatial, but not all Tulsa's citizens were so fortunate. Throngs of dream-seekers lived in poverty still searching for fortune. Tulsa's crime wave got out of hand. Prostitution and bootlegging fueled the mix often bringing the inevitable clash between the desires of the wealthy and the willingness to satiate those desires by those less fortunate. The two sides of the tracks fed each other and fueled the fire.

North of the light-skinned throngs, Greenwood sprang up, almost unnoticed at first. Greenwood was a close-knit community of approximately 10,000 African Americans. Some of them had arrived with Native Americans at the end of the Trail of Tears, some had travelled to Tulsa to escape discrimination left over from the days of slavery, and still others had come in search of fortune.

Many of them found their dreams. Some struck oil, but most merely took advantage of the opportunity to turn hard work into cold cash. Jim Crow laws prevented them from shopping in the white businesses of Tulsa, so entrepreneurs turned this fact into advantage and built their own shops.

Money that filtered into Greenwood from workers in white Tulsa stayed in Greenwood. They spent their money with their own. In a relatively short time, many Greenwood residents enjoyed such prosperity that they became known as "Black Wall Street." They were living the American Dream.

Some of the successful residents built fine homes and businesses and furnished them with expensive imported furnishings. Grand pianos and diamond necklaces were not rare in

Greenwood, but white faces were. Unsuccessful dream-seekers in Tulsa envied the wealth of Greenwood to such a degree that the envy was certain to spill over into violence.

Greenwood had its own hospital and fifteen physicians, including a nationally renowned surgeon. They also had a library, a school, two theaters, and most any other service residents needed. Anywhere a need arose, an entrepreneur stepped up to fill the need. Shortly before the riot, Greenwood residents had just completed a fine new church built of bricks and mortar. They had two handsome hotels. All of this was a source of pride for everyone in Greenwood, but they apparently were also a source of hatred for some Tulsans.

CHAPTER 2

DICK ROWLAND

I could see disaster coming down the tracks, but I still rode the train. As a city boy, I mixed easily with both sides of the tracks and came to know many of the Greenwood residents personally. Dick Rowland was one of those residents. He was purported to be the root of the problem on Memorial Day, but he was far from wealthy. The first time I talked to Dick, he was shining shoes at a shoe-shine stand near the Drexel Building downtown. I stopped in for a shine on a hot summer day in 1920.

Dick was finishing up a shine for the mayor. He popped his rag with a smart snap and grinned as the mayor patted his back and pressed two coins in Dick's hand, one for Dick and one for Dick's boss who was watching from his tidy desk inside his office. Dick's chair was set up under an overhang in front of the brick façade of the establishment to take advantage of the scant breeze blowing down the street. The air was barely moving and smelled of dust and shoe polish. Dick swiped a mostly clean rag across the chair and said, "Sit right up here, mister, and I'll fix you up with the best shine you ever had."

I tucked my newspaper under my arm and sat down. Dick began to rub a little polish on my boots and hum a familiar tune under his breath. I studied his face while he worked. It was a roadmap. He kept to himself, but a journalist always looks for the hidden story. I saw one in his eyes. I asked his name.

"Dick, sir. My name's Dick," he replied.

"Well, Dick. I'm Sam. Pleased to meet you," I responded.

"Thank you, sir. I'll fix these fine boots right up for you. Best shine in town, that's what you'll get." He worked all the while, never making eye contact with me, but I didn't take my eyes off him.

"That's what I hear. Rumor is you are the best," I continued.

Dick chuckled and said, "They'd be right, sir. I'm the best shine boy in town."

"How old are you, boy?" I asked.

"Eighteen, sir."

"You been doing this long?"

"All my life, seems like. Started when I was about 10, I reckon." Still he kept his head down and his eyes on my boots.

"Your folks send you out to work?"

"No sir, I don't really have any folks. Miss Damie, she took me in, but my folks been gone since I was five or six. Don't remember much about them."

"Oh," I responded. "Didn't I see you playing football at the high school a couple of years ago?"

"Yes sir. I was good too. But playing football didn't put food in my belly, so I had to let that be and get to doing something that paid a little better," said Dick with a broad smile. Finally he looked at me.

By then he was snapping the rag once again. When he finished, he stood up and glanced at the man behind the glass in the office. His expression changed to less than a smile. He looked back down at his own feet. I understood. His own well-worn shoes were spotless, and his tired shirt was clean and neatly pressed. The collar was tattered at the creases but it was still stiff and pressed. His long fingers clutched the can of polish, and he glanced again at the man behind the glass. He shifted his weight from one foot to the other. I got the message.

I put two shiny coins in his hand and said, "Well Dick, looks like we'll have to continue this conversation when my boots get dirty again."

Dick laughed and nodded. He looked at me one last time, and his eyes reminded me of a child. They were wide and fringed with the longest eyelashes I think I have ever seen. He was very dark even for a Greenwood man, and his face seemed both young and old at the same time. The next man waiting for a shine stepped up and took the seat I vacated. I tipped my hat to Dick and nodded to the man behind the glass. He never smiled but nodded. Dick Rowland would be referred to later by the *Tulsa Tribune* as "Diamond Dick," indicating a flashy cad, but this was about as far as I could imagine from the shy young man I met that day.

My encounter with Rowland heightened my curiosity about Greenwood. It was a fine spring day, so I strolled down toward Greenwood. I soon found myself on Greenwood Avenue. I passed countless shops. Each one seemed to have a back story of its own. Curiosity killed the cat, and I figured one day it would get me too. Greenwood held a certain fascination for me. I wanted to understand what I recognized as a phenomenon. There was an intangible energy among the people. They bustled about as if their roles had been scripted for a Broadway show.

Three well-behaved children passed me, the boys in gray suits with short pants and neatly tied silk ascots tucked into crisp white shirts. The small girl wore silk with ruffles and lace. She carried a parasol with the grace of a ballerina. She couldn't have been more than eight years old. They paused in front of a hat shop to wait for their mother, who came out presently and said to the children, "Come along. Papa is waiting." She wore a deep red silk dress and hat and carried herself with sophisticated poise similar to that of her tiny daughter. She was a lady, a lady with caramel skin and rubies dangling from her ear lobes. A long string of pearls hung about her thin neck, draped twice around.

I had to smile as they walked away from me with a rustle of silk, the children following their mother as ducklings follow a swan. I never knew who they were, but I have often wondered what became of them. They should have all become swans with rubies and pearls.

CHAPTER 3

O.W. GURLEY

One of the first Greenwood residents I met was the founder of the town, O. W. Gurley. I bumped into Gurley one afternoon in front of his hotel. The Gurley Hotel and Billiard Parlor was at the center of town. No one could miss it. The façade smacked of money, and money bags himself was standing out front with the biggest cigar I had ever seen hanging from his lips. He puffed and blew smoke into the air as if he owned the very atmosphere. "Top of the morning to you, Mr. Gurley," I said as I approached him.

"And to you sir," he replied, "But I don't believe I've had the pleasure. Do I know you?"

I laughed at my own arrogance. "No sir, I doubt you do. I work for the *Tulsa World*. I'm one of those nosey reporters you complain about in the *Star*."

Now it was his turn to laugh. "Ah, I see. And you've come to find out if I really am the big blow hard you believe me to be."

I wasn't quite sure how he intended that comment, so I smiled but was caught a bit off guard. He could see my discomfiture, so being the consummate gentleman, he added,

"Please come in and see for yourself, Mr. what did you say your name was?"

"Sam, Sam Stackhouse, Mr. Gurley. Everyone knows who you are, but I'm afraid I don't share that notoriety."

"Well Sam, Mr. Stackhouse, come inside, and I'll personally buy you a tall lemonade. Then you can decide." With that and a sweeping gesture of his hand, he invited me into his hotel.

I expected to see gaudy red drapes and gilded furniture perhaps more like a cat house than a hotel, but instead I saw classic Victorian furniture tastefully upholstered in conservative blue velvet. Fine Tiffany lamps glowed softly as ladies with parasols and silk dresses quietly read by their light. A tall black man was playing a Beethoven piece on a Steinway grand piano sitting in the far corner of the lobby. The soft music and glowing lamps gave a serene atmosphere to the room. I was stunned.

Gurley bowed his head slightly, probably to hide the smirk on his face. "I see you approve of my choice of music. Rufus has been playing here every day since we opened. Feel free to make any request you like. It might surprise you how many tunes he can play from memory. The strangest thing is that he doesn't read a note of music, plays it all by ear. Come this way. We can sit in the lounge for a chat."

I followed him obediently, mesmerized by what I saw and heard. My amazement must have given me away, but gentleman that he was, he never appeared to notice. I was the only white face in the building, but no one seemed unsettled by that fact except me. People I passed nodded politely and went about their business. Gurley led me to a pair of comfortable leather chairs in the back of the lounge area. As soon as we sat down, a white-gloved waiter appeared as if by magic and asked Mr. Gurley if he could bring us anything.

Gurley's voice was soft and low. He ordered two lemonades and winked at the waiter. The waiter smiled and nodded. He disappeared as quietly as he had arrived and soon returned with two tall glasses. He set one down in front of each one of us. He placed them on silver coasters with a faint "G" engraved in the center. The room was dimly lit and slender candles flickered in front of small mirrored sconces placed strategically on the walls around the perimeter of the room. I lifted my glass to salute my host while the flickering flame reflected on the glass like an etched ruby.

I sipped my drink slowly. I had been outside for a while and was quite parched, so the idea of lemonade was most welcome. I knew immediately why the waiter had smiled. This was not all lemonade. "Ah," I said. "I see you are a man of fine taste, indeed."

"We try, Mr. Stackhouse, we try," Gurley replied.

"Mr. Gurley, you obviously have been very successful in Greenwood. Have you always lived in the area?" I asked.

"No, I came here in 1906. I had been in Arkansas and sold some land for a nice profit, so I thought I'd try my luck here in Oklahoma. I thought maybe I'd manage to buy some land with oil beneath its surface, but it appears I might have missed the mark on that goal. I bought 40 acres and opened a boarding house since it presented some difficulty for people of color to find lodging in these parts. Many people were arriving here to work in the oil fields and needed a place to stay, so I figured I might as well provide that service. It was a small property located on a dusty road, but it did quite well. Then I ventured out and built three office buildings where doctors, lawyers, dentists, and realtors could set up shop. Later we added barbershops and beauty salons to take care of the tenants. Those ventures proved to be good investments and provided me with the capital to build this hotel. As you can see, we have a rather tame clientele, but they pay the bills."

Gurley's description of his businesses was certainly understated. He was far more successful than anyone I knew, yet he downplayed his success at every turn. Later, he was to use this same reserve and good judgment in his response to the riot, but he still sustained huge losses, including his beautiful hotel where we enjoyed the "lemonade."

"I must admit, this visit has been most enjoyable. I do hope I may be invited back again," I said.

"Why certainly. You are most welcome any time. Feel free to join us when you are in the area," Gurley replied politely.

I studied his face as he spoke to me, and it occurred to me that I could not offer to return his hospitality. I wondered if he might be thinking the same thing. I stumbled a bit with my response. "I hope to take you up on that. I'd love to extend the same courtesy to you, but I'm afraid you would find my meager accommodations not suitable. I live in a small room in a boarding house on Washington Avenue."

Gurley put his hand on my shoulder and replied, "Thank you very much, Sam. I appreciate your thoughts. I assure you that your surroundings would not be unpleasant to me, but you must realize that visit cannot take place."

I said nothing but offered my hand and looked him squarely in the eye, a glance which he returned. We both understood and were for a moment only two men shaking hands upon parting from a pleasant respite from the world.

I walked out the door and started down the walkway, thinking about our exchange. The difference between Gurley and me didn't seem as important as it had earlier. He was older and had much more money than I did, but so did most people I knew. I passed shop after shop on Greenwood then on Hartfort. People greeted me as I passed them. Shop owners sometimes looked up as I passed their doors. How odd I must look to them. They must think me to be a curiosity.

When I walked by the Stradford Hotel, I wondered how it compared to Gurley's hotel, but I was never to find out. It was much larger and had a grand façade, so I wondered if it had similar charm. It was in the heart of Greenwood. I heard it boasted of 65 rooms and had opened its doors just recently on June 1, 1918, not so long before I arrived on the scene. Three years later to the day would be an anniversary that would haunt Stradford for the rest of his life. He was born the son of a freed slave in Kentucky before the Civil War ended, and he rose to become the wealthiest man in Greenwood. He managed to graduate from Oberlin College then went to law school in Indiana. He and his wife Augusta thrived in Tulsa until the riot.

I walked past so many interesting places that day and I don't think my life was ever quite the same again. Thomas Wolfe said "Every moment is a window on all time," and this is what I felt. This was a window in time. I ambled past Doc's Beanery and Hamburger Kelly's place then saw Lilly Johnson's Liberty Café. I peered in through the gaily painted window and saw neat tables laid with red and white checked table cloths. On each one was a glass with a fresh flower in it. People inside chatted and laughed while they shoveled food into their mouths. The food looked like somebody's mother had cooked it. They were obviously enjoying their meals. I wanted to join them, but I was afraid a white dot in the midst of this gaiety might dampen the feeling, so I kept walking. One man dining near the window caught me looking in and frowned. He quickly averted his face and continued his meal. Mable Little's beauty shop was next, then I was tempted by Rolly and Ada Huff's confectionery on Archer. A sign out front advertised Coca-Cola and sarsaparilla. Again I was tempted, but I kept walking.

Maybe the Dreamland Theater got more of my attention than anything except the Stradford. I had heard about the Williams family from some of the fellows I worked with. Williams was a true entrepreneur. His entire family worked together to create significant wealth. He owned the first automobile in Greenwood and became so adept at keeping it running that he opened up a garage to repair cars other residents bought. The theater hosted silent movies and musical revues. I was sure I would enjoy many of their performances, but again, I didn't want to be the white dot.

Greenwood was a close-knit group of perhaps 10,000 citizens. They kept their business quiet and within their own borders so money that came into the town from jobs in the white sector of Tulsa re-circulated only in Greenwood. This practice soon built a group like no other. Many of them were so successful they owned fine European furnishings for their elaborate homes and drove cars and wore jewelry far superior to most of their lighter-skinned Tulsa counterparts. At their peak, they had 21 churches, 30 grocery stores, two movie theaters, a bank, a hospital, a post office, and a library all for their own use, and they had a bus system to transport them through the town. But success like this does not go unnoticed, nor is it appreciated by those who do not benefit from it.

CHAPTER 4

ROY BELTON

Kept secret for years, it was problems in white Tulsa that began the string of events leading to the Memorial Day Riot. With the huge success of Tulsa came huge problems. Where that much money circulates, men (and women) will come looking for it. That is where Roy Belton comes in. Belton and his lady friend took a ride in Homer Nida's taxi one night, and Nida came out on the raw end of the deal. This was big news, and I was assigned to cover the story.

Belton was arrested after Nida, who was still in the hospital, identified him as the man who shot him. The *Tulsa Tribune*, always looking for a sensational lead, published Belton's picture and began to stir the pot. They suggested the idea of a lynching even before Nida died. When he died, they stoked the fire even more.

Belton was eighteen years old, and he wanted more, lots more. He wasn't exactly inclined to work, so he found another way to get what he wanted. I collected my facts then went to the jail to talk to Belton. The county jail was on the top floor of the grand new courthouse. It was a sturdy stone structure, and it made sense to put the jail in the same building with the courts so prisoners couldn't escape as they were being brought to court, but that was assuming officials in charge would do their job properly. It was the wild, wild West in those days, so how the job was done was often a matter of opinion rather than law.

Belton was in a cell when I first saw him. He looked like he was sobering up from a long drunk, and maybe he was. Liquor and drugs flowed freely through the streets of Tulsa, and Belton liked both. He wasn't a big guy, just average size, and he had this scraggly looking sandy blond hair sticking out in all directions. He was dirty, and his clothes indicated he had slept in them for more than one night. I smelled him before I saw him. The cell was dim, but one shaft of light came through the bars on the window like a spotlight and made a silhouette of Belton's body. I held my pad and pencil in my hand and introduced myself. Belton was a bit awkward at first.

"What you want with me?" he asked.

"I'd like to hear your side of this story. Is it true that you admitted to shooting Nida?"

"Yeah, what's it to you? He shoulda just handed me the money, and I wouldn't a hurt him none. He just had to show off. He shoved me. I just defended myself. I couldn't let him do that in front of my woman. He had plenty money. I saw it. I needed it. Me and my woman, we didn't have no place to stay. We needed that money, and he could make some more," Belton insisted, then he added. "Hey man, you got a cigarette on you?"

I pulled a pack of Camel's out of my pocket and flipped the package so one popped up, "So you shot him because he wouldn't give you his money?"

Belton grabbed the cigarette from the pack and said, "No, man. I shot him because he shoved me. It was self defense. Yeah, that's what it was. But he shoulda give me the money, too. They ain't going to convict me cause I was just defending myself.

18

Anyway if that don't work, I know how to act real crazy," Belton said, then he began to dance around and make monkey sounds. "Hey, man. You got a light," he added.

I had my doubts about him, but he was crazy, crazy like a fox. This was not his first brush with the law. I had checked with Sheriff Wooley before I went to his cell. I knew he'd been in trouble since he was 13 years old. I could see this was going nowhere, so I called for the deputy to let me out. The deputy spat his wad of tobacco into a nearby spittoon and rattled his keys in front of the cell like a kid with candy. The deputy and the inmate were two sides of the same coin.

Belton shouted after me, "Hey, man, you didn't give me no light. What you want me to do with this thing? Eat it?"

I kept walking down the corridor, listening to the monkey sounds again. The deputy shouted, "Shut up or I'll come in there and shut you up. You aint' no monkey—you just stupid like a monkey!"

Later that night I saw the true colors of that deputy and perhaps the town or maybe even the country at that time. I stopped in the barbershop that afternoon and heard rumblings of a lynching if Nida died, so I knew this was a volatile situation. An abandoned copy of the *Tribune* was draped across the arm of an empty chair and several men were gathered in front of the barbershop. I pretended to read my paper and listened. Some talked about what a good man Nida was. Others indicated they should "take care of business" themselves. It all seemed to hinge on Nida's life or death, but I wasn't sure Belton was safe either way. One of the men shook his copy of the *Tribune* and read from it. He said, "It's right here in plain print: 'Belton plans to escape on a plea of insanity.'"

This was a stretch even for the *Tribune*. Belton must have said the same thing to the *Tribune* reporter that he had said to me. Unfortunately, they took him seriously or at least pretended to. The men were interrupted in mid sentence by an excited man rushing up to them and saying, "He died! Nida died. His wife is outside the hospital right now saying we got to do justice to her husband."

One large man stood up and straightened his britches over his cowboy boots then stuffed his Stetson hat on his head and said, "Well, boys, I guess you know what we got to do now." He walked away, leaving the men to stare after him in a deathly quiet room. The group rushed after him like puppies following their mother's teat. I headed for this hospital. By the time I got there, the grieving widow was on the steps speaking to the gathering crowd.

Mrs. Nida was a squat woman, low to the ground, with streaks of gray in her dark hair. She straightened her dress and stood as tall as she could. Anger, not grief, broke her voice. She swore under her breath then shouted, "I hope that justice will be done for they have taken an innocent life and ruined my happiness. They deserve to be mobbed—but the other way is better." Then she pointed toward the taxi where the murder had taken place, insisting that her husband didn't deserve his fate. The taxi became a symbol.

None of the men in the crowd actually knew Nida. They were hungry for justice, vigilante justice. The man in the Stetson stepped up to take Mrs. Nida's arm. He leaned down and whispered in her ear. She looked up at him with her eyes wide and her mouth open. She pulled a key from her pocket. With a trembling hand, she laid the key in his large calloused hand. He doffed his hat and moved toward the crowd while the stunned woman watched. He gestured to his buddies and opened the door of the taxi to the cheers of the waiting crowd. Three of the men got into the taxi with the Stetson. Men began to run to their cars. Engines roared, and soon the entourage sped off toward the courthouse. They halted abruptly in front of the courthouse. The Stetson stepped out of the taxi and became a beacon for the mob.

I followed the crowd and was standing on the steps when the Stetson went inside. I slipped in a side door and raced up the stairs while the Stetson and his posse went up on the elevator. I reached the top just as the elevator door opened.

The Stetson bellowed, "Wooley, we come to get him. Hand him over!" One of the men had a clearly visible nickel-plated pistol tucked into his belt, one brandished a leather-bound billy club, and the third rattled a pair of police-issue hand cuffs. They marched into Wooley's office. Wooley stood up and snatched the cell keys from the wall.

"Settle down, boys. You know we can't do that. He'll get a trial. We'll hang him, but we gotta go through the motions," Wooley said, clutching the keys. Suddenly he laid the keys on the desk and continued, "Course, I couldn't do nothin' about it if you boys was to overpower me."

His wide grin exposed a gap where someone had most likely knocked out one of his front teeth. The Stetson picked up the keys and said, "Sheb you hold the sheriff's arms while I take care of business." Sheb laid the billy club where the keys had been, and the Stetson disappeared down the corridor.

We all heard Belton scream and an iron door slam shut. The Stetson reappeared holding Belton's arms behind him. Belton appeared much smaller and younger than he had the day before when he sat in his cell striped by the sunlight. The man with the hand cuffs snapped them onto Belton's hands and shoved him toward the elevator. They seemed oblivious to my presence. No one would interfere with them. A deputy came out of the restroom about this time and looked at Wooley then at Belton. Wooley smiled, and the deputy walked back in the restroom without saying a word.

The Stetson nodded to Wooley and went to the elevator. Sheb let go of Wooley's arm and tipped his hat. Wooley never rose from his desk. He said as they were leaving, "You boys watch out now. I'll make sure don't nobody bother you." Then he reached for his phone and made two calls.

It was dark outside by the time the courthouse doors burst open and the Stetson and his entourage emerged. The doors slammed shut behind them just as I slipped out the side door where I had entered unnoticed a few minutes earlier. The Stetson held Belton by his shirt collar as he shuffled him down the steps and across the street to Nida's taxi. Then he stuffed Belton in the back seat of the taxi. Two of the men got in the back seat with him and the other in the front with the Stetson. The Stetson got in the driver's seat, and they roared off down the street. They headed out the road to Jenks, which is about nine miles from Tulsa. I fell in line in the procession. By the time we got to the edge of town, police cars were lined up directing traffic so the flow of the snake would not be interrupted. Two cars with sheriff's department logos on the doors joined in. When we got just outside Jenks, the Stetson pulled the taxi off the road and stopped. A massive tree formed a canopy over the road. It had sturdy branches. The Stetson walked over to a limb about 10 feet off the ground and threw a rope over the branch. "Sheb, bring him over here. George, park Nida's taxi right here," said the Stetson, motioning to a spot directly beneath the limb.

Sheb shoved Belton toward the Stetson as two men began looping a hangman's noose in the end of the rope. Their laughter echoed through the surrounding pastures, and flasks of hooch appeared as if by magic. The taxi was positioned directly beneath the tree. The Stetson directed one man to put the loop around Belton's neck and the other to jump up on the hood of the Taxi. Then they shoved a screaming, pleading Belton onto the hood. The crowd began to hoist the man to his feet. Belton was standing on the hood of the car when it lunged backward, leaving Belton swinging from the tree. After a while the swinging stopped and Belton was still, but the crowd was not. They shouted and jeered as police kept order and directed traffic.

CHAPTER 5

A.J. SMITHERMAN

This incident was duly noted by the *World* and the *Tribune*, but neither viewed it with quite the same eyes as the *Star*. The *Star* was owned and operated by Andrew J. Smitherman. I considered it an absolute necessity to read my competition daily, and I soon became alarmed by the editorials I saw in the *Star*. While the *Tribune* stirred the pot to the south of the tracks, the *Star* was doing the same to the north. One of them used the incident to increase its customer base. The other used it to warn readers of a dark future. Both accomplished their goals.

I saw myself as the noble journalist, interested in truth, but some days it was difficult to find that illusive entity. Smitherman made the point quite clearly that if white Tulsans would lynch one of their own with such blatant assistance from the office of men appointed to protect its citizens, then surely no person of color stood a chance in any similar situation. He insisted that if such circumstances arose, the men of Greenwood must stand together and protect their own. Many of those men had served honorably in World War I, so they knew how to fight and believed they had as

much right to live free and prosper as lighter-skinned neighbors.
The only thing protecting them from backlash after these editorials
was the fact that their light-skinned neighbors did not read the *Star*.

Since I had grown up in a diverse neighborhood in the city
and I knew Smitherman's background, I took his journalistic rants
a bit more seriously than did my cohorts, who mostly preferred to
pretend that Smitherman did not exist or that his opinions had no
value. And then there was the curiosity problem. That curiosity
once again lured me into trouble when I decided to make it my
business to know more about the infamous A. J. Smitherman.

I sauntered along Greenwood Avenue one afternoon,
oblivious to how much I stood out against the crowd. When I
reached the front door of the *Star*, I paused. The wide glass
window was marked with carefully painted gold lettering. I
straightened my collar and opened the heavy leaded glass door. It
made no sound as it swung open. A well-dressed receptionist sat
behind a desk near the front door and looked up from her work to
address me: "May I help you, sir?"

I walked over to the raised counter in front of her and
propped one elbow on the polished wood. She was quite attractive
and smiled pleasantly at me. Her hair fell in soft curls about her
face, and her eyes were soft and genuine. I always judged a woman
by her eyes. "Yes, ma'am. You certainly may, or at least I hope so.
Would the esteemed Mr. A. J. Smitherman be in at the moment?"

"Let me check for you, sir. May I have your name and the
nature of your business?"

"Yes ma'am. My name is Sam Stackhouse. I'm a reporter
for the *Tulsa World*, and I would like to speak to Mr. Smitherman
if you can arrange that," I answered. She smiled at my attempted
banter and nodded.

She stood up and straightened her fine gray wool skirt then
walked to a door at the far side of the room. She wore a crisp white
blouse with pearl buttons and had a wide red leather belt cinched
around her tiny waist. She wore a long single strand of pearls,

which she had looped into a knot that dangled above the belt. Watching her walk across the room, I was surprised at her polish and grace. I'm not sure what I was expecting, but she wasn't it. The door was closed but she tapped lightly then entered without a sound. I heard soft voices coming from the room, then she emerged and returned to her desk. "Mr. Smitherman will see you now."

When I stepped into the office, Smitherman was seated behind a mahogany desk. He looked up from a stack of papers in front of him and removed his glasses, setting them down neatly on top of the stack. Then he leaned back in his chair and said, "What can I do for you, Mr. Stackhouse?"

I could see that he was assessing me carefully. "I would like a few minutes of your time, Mr. Smitherman. I've been reading your editorials and would like to talk about some of your statements." I carefully monitored my tone so he could not read my reasons. The truth is, I'm still not sure what my reasons were other than curiosity.

Smitherman laughed politely and replied, "So, I've ruffled your journalistic feathers, have I? Please have a seat, Mr. Stackhouse." As I sat down, he continued, "You're not from around here are you, Mr. Stackhouse?"

I tried to keep my mouth from curling into that lopsided grin that comes over me when I'm nervous and answered, "What gives me away?"

"Everything, Mr. Stackhouse, everything."

"Well, no, I'm a city boy. New to Oklahoma," I responded.

"And what brought you here?" he asked.

"Oh, I don't know. When my mother died, it just seemed the right thing to do. I got on a train headed west and got off when I got tired of riding. So here I am."

"And your father, where is he?" Smitherman asked.

"I have no idea. He was a riverboat gambler without a riverboat. He moved on when I was a baby."

"And you, Mr. Stackhouse, are you a riverboat gambler?" Smitherman asked. He was the quintessential journalist, questioning everything.

The grin came on in spite of all I could do. "Maybe so. Maybe that's why I'm here sitting in front of my betters, trying to learn," I told him.

Now it was Smitherman's turn to smile. I had finally broken through the wall that was his face. "Ok, Mr. Stackhouse, what really brings you here? But before you answer, you should know that I've probably read everything you've written since you arrived in Tulsa."

"Curiosity lured me here, but now it's worse. You actually read my stories? I'm very flattered."

"Don't be, Mr. Stackhouse. I read the entire *World* and *Tribune* every day the sun comes up. How else can I know the pulse of the community? I assume you do the same?"

"Well, maybe not *every* word, but most. I assume you know sometimes your words leak across the tracks, and certain people may not take them well. That being said, I admire your honesty. Apparently the governor does, too. I understand you are going to be meeting with the governor's committee on race relations shortly. Did that invitation or even the existence of the committee surprise you?"

"Mr. Stackhouse, if I didn't write articles that some readers *don't take well*, I would not call myself a journalist, and as for the invitation, no, I'm not surprised."

"No offense, Mr. Smitherman. Perhaps I'm not as well informed as I believed myself to be." Suddenly the tone of our conversation had put on white gloves. The air between us was pushing me out the door.

Being the consummate barrister, Smitherman reached out. "None taken, Mr. Stackhouse. And perhaps you didn't know I am a lawyer, so it is my business not only to know about such things, but to make sure others know as well. Relax, Mr. Stackhouse. The fact that you are here says you look for truth. What exactly is it that you seek to find out about me?"

I took a deep breath and settled back into my chair. I studied Smitherman's face for as long as I dared then hesitated a moment more. His skin indicated a probable connection to the Native Americans who arrived in Oklahoma via the Trail of Tears, but I thought best not to question his parentage, so I began with his education. "I suppose *everything* would be a bit too broad. How about we start with how did you get here, to Greenwood, I mean? I assume you received your education in the north."

"You are correct. I was born in Alabama but moved to Indian Territory in the 90's then attended the University of Kansas. Later I received a law degree from LaSalle University in Philadelphia. As for my invitation, the state house is certainly aware of my presence and has been for a while. It is not my way to remain silent when words or actions are needed. Silence serves no one well. Three years ago an angry mob of white people burned twenty homes of my people. Local law enforcement seemed unwilling to help them, so I went to the statehouse and reported the episode directly to Governor Williams. Consequently thirty-six white men were arrested, including the mayor of the town. This is the kind of thing the NAACP strives to do. You are aware of that organization, I presume."

"Yes, I am, but I admit that I have not heard the term issued from smiling lips. You are a member of that group?" I asked.

"Certainly. I was there when it was founded." Smitherman picked up a copy of a publication called *The Crisis*. "This, my friend," he said, "is the fruit of that group of concerned Americans. We strive to make this country free and safe for all its citizens, not just those with pale faces."

I took the magazine from him and flipped through its pages. The names I saw in the magazine surprised me. The one that struck me most was Langston Hughes. "Do you know Langston Hughes, Mr. Smitherman?"

"As a matter of fact, I do. He is a fine poet and works diligently for our cause. He lives and works in Harlem. Have you ever been to Harlem, Mr. Stackhouse? I assume not."

I laughed heartily, "Now it is my turn to surprise you, Mr. Smitherman. Yes, I'm quite familiar with Harlem. When I worked in the city, I covered events in Harlem on a regular basis. I quite enjoyed the music and poetry I heard there, but I was never fortunate enough to rub shoulders with Mr. Hughes. I would have considered that the ultimate privilege."

"You do surprise me, young man. So you wrote of issues relating to Harlem in a white newspaper?"

"No, not really. I covered the arts. The music and art seeping out of Harlem is hard to resist, and there is a certain segment of the city that prides itself in being, shall we say, progressive? The village takes great pride in its forward motion. I'm not sure they know why, but they do. They like to opine about matters of which they have little knowledge and even less experience."

"And you, do you have *experience*?" Smitherman asked, looking deeply into my face.

"Some. Can we talk man-to-man, Mr. Smitherman?" I asked.

"I assumed that is what we were doing, Mr. Stackhouse. Is it not?" Smitherman challenged me with one eyebrow raised.

Ignoring his jab, I said, "I want to know what makes you tick. I'd like to hear your thoughts about the real issues we are dancing around, Mr. Smitherman. Tell me what you are about. I think I have a pretty good idea, but I want to hear your story. And please, can you call me Sam?"

Now Smitherman settled back into his chair and took a cigar from a simple teakwood box. Extending the open box to me, he asked, "Care to join me, Sam?"

"Don't mind if I do, Mr. Smitherman," I replied looking straight into his eyes rather than at the cigar in my hand.

"A. J." he said quietly.

Then he began, "You are aware, I assume, that I forced the issue of a separate voting ward for Greenwood and that I am the inspector of elections. Without real voting rights, nothing can ever change. That is where we had to begin. Of course, we could never have secured that right without money. You may look around and see much wealth and perhaps envy the luxury many citizens of Greenwood enjoy, but that wealth did not fall into our pockets by chance, and many of us do not flaunt the privilege. But we had to amass this bankroll before we could live like human beings. Animals, they have called us. Monkeys without tails, jigaboos, niggers. When our ancestors were brought over on slave ships, few knew the white man's words, none had homes or money, all were frightened, and none had any idea what the future would bring. They were whipped into a role that some would have them fill even today. Do you understand how many lynchings have taken place over the years? How many human beings have lost their lives, some for infractions as simple as looking at a white woman? The hysteria swirling in this country over the imagined uncontrollable desire Negro men have to bed white women is as pernicious as hemlock. One whiff of it and a man dies. No proof is needed, just the perception."

I looked around me at the simple surroundings in this office. Rows of files lined the walls, simple maps hung above the files, a large desk anchored the center of the room, and a small, quiet man ruled benevolently but powerfully from his simple throne. I saw a man. One silver framed photo sat on his desk among the stacks of papers. The photo was of a handsome dark-skinned woman and five lighter-skinned children who appeared to be stepping stones one to two years apart in age. The woman was elegant in her mien and dress. The children were clad in fine suits and ruffled dresses with bows in their hair. I didn't know how to answer his diatribe.

"A. J., why do you think this hysteria continues? There

must be a reason," I asked.

"It didn't start without cause, but the cause may be quite different from what you imagine," Smitherman replied.

"You don't think there is any validity to the urge of one race to mate with the other, I assume."

"Do you?" Smitherman countered.

I squirmed in my seat and mumbled.

Smitherman laughed. "Yes, I thought so. As a part of my law degree, I studied psychology, the science of human behavior, and we are all humans, you know. We are all governed to some degree by fear of the unknown. How much do you think you know about me and my family? How many times have you visited a home in Greenwood? How well do you think slave owners knew their slaves? Did you know that if you cut open my chest, you will find that I bleed the same color blood you bleed or that my heart will be indistinguishable from yours? Many of my race are larger than some of your race just as many yellow-skinned men are smaller on average than your race. Size generally gives a man advantage, wouldn't you agree?"

"Yes, I suppose it does, but other things give us power."

"Really? What gives us power over others?" Smitherman leaned forward bringing his face closer to mine. The whites of his eyes seemed to glow.

"Money."

"How about laws and governments? Do they empower one class over another?"

"Of course."

"And how does that happen? Who makes laws? What are they designed to do?" Smitherman continued.

I shifted my weight to one side and propped myself on the smooth leather arm of my chair. Smitherman laughed and relaxed his pose once again. "I'm not attacking you, Sam. Relax. I'm merely trying to get you to see the power structure we all operate under. Each man must grab his own stick and use it. African ancestry often dictates taller, more powerful, dark skinned individuals. The climate of Africa is such that these attributes facilitate survival. Unfortunately today in this country, those very traits often dictate destruction. Think about this: when men of smaller physical stature can accumulate money and legal power, they can legislate their own rules. Man always seeks ruling power over those he fears or does not understand. White men fear men of African heritage because of their physical prowess, and since they perceive their women to be the epitome of beauty, why would they not think everyone would desire their women. But they forget that each man perceives beauty in his own terms. To me, my wife is the most beautiful of all women. She has a grace and beauty that won my heart the first moment I laid eyes on her. But should I assume you would desire my wife if you were to meet her?"

I cocked my head to the side and gave him that crooked smile then countered, "Does this mean I won't get an invitation to your home?"

Now Smitherman laughed heartily. "On the contrary, my new friend. You have earned that right by coming here today and allowing me the privilege of an intellectual tirade, my specialty. Dinner is at 8:00. I shall call my wife now and inform her that we have an additional guest. Unfortunately we will have to continue our discussion at that time, for I have another appointment very shortly." Smitherman stood up and motioned toward the door. "It has been a real pleasure, Sam. I hope this is the first of many discussions for us." He handed me a gold embossed card with his address on it.

I took the card and extended my hand to Smitherman. "You can count on it, A. J. I can see that I'm outwitted, but maybe I can learn from the master. I'll see you at 8:00."

The receptionist was still at her desk when I walked out. She smiled at me and said, "Good day, Mr. Stackhouse."

"Thank you, Melanie. Good day to you as well. I hope we shall meet again," I said to her. Had her skin been lighter, I think I would have seen a blush. Her name plate gave me her name, but I think I caught her off-guard. I recalled the recent conversation with her boss about desires between the races and chuckled to myself as I walked out the door. She really was a lovely girl.

I arrived at the Smitherman home promptly at 8:00 with flowers and a box of chocolates for Mrs. Smitherman. The home spoke of quality but not pretention. I rapped on the front door. It was opened promptly by a white-gloved butler. He was over six feet tall and powerfully built in contrast to Smitherman whose build was slight and whose voice was quiet, which I was to learn later was not always the case. "Please come in Mr. Stackhouse. Mr. Smitherman is expecting you."

I was ushered into a formal dining room with a long table laid with fine linens and crystal glasses. Even the china and silver indicated taste, refinement and, most of all, money. Pink roses were skillfully arranged in the center of the table and flanked on either side by tall silver candelabra. The dining room had a salon area at the far end next to a gracefully draped bow window. Six men and their wives were milling around chatting near the window. Cream colored velvet panels fell in perfect folds from the tops of the tall windows and gave a hush to the room. The group was engrossed in conversation as the butler cleared his throat and announced: "Mr. Samuel Stackhouse."

I don't think I've ever had my presence announced in a room before so I felt a bit ill at ease, but ever the elegant host, Smitherman responded, "Thank you, Johnson. That will be all. Please join us Sam. We were just discussing the news of the day. You must have something to add to that mix." He motioned for me to join them.

A very beautiful woman stood by his side. He introduced her first, "Sam, this is my wife, Ollie."

I was stunned by her presence. She smiled softly and looked directly into my eyes when she spoke, "We are so pleased you could join us tonight. A. J. has told me how much he enjoyed talking to you today."

I felt like a school boy staring at the most beautiful girl in the school and trying to speak. I knew whatever I said would not be adequate, so I handed her the flowers and candy and said, "Thank you for inviting me into your home. I hope you like daisies. The florist said they were fresh and should hold up well." Ok, now I'm officially marked as an idiot. What do you say in a situation like this?

With the grace of a princess, Mrs. Smitherman replied, "How ever did you know that daisies were my favorite, Mr. Stackhouse? They are lovely, and is that chocolate you are holding? If that is for me, I must stash it away to keep it from A. J., or I shall never even get a taste. Johnson, please come and put these lovely daisies in a vase for me."

I let out a sigh of relief, which didn't go unnoticed. A. J. took my arm and laughed. "See, I told you she was beautiful, didn't I?"

"Well you certainly didn't lie about that!" I replied.

"Come let me introduce you. O.W., this is Sam Stackhouse."

Mr. Gurley quickly noted, "Nice to see you, Sam. Sam and I met several months ago. He is quite the inquisitive reporter, but not a bad chap. Sam, this is my friend, B. C. Franklin, and this distinguished gentleman is Dr. A. C. Jackson."

About that time Johnson arrived with a tall vase with the daisies arranged in it. He bent low to whisper in Mrs. Smitherman's ear. She motioned to the server holding a silver bowl filled with punch (something like the "lemonade" I had enjoyed at Gurley's hotel). He set the vase down beside the bowl then disappeared.

Smitherman ushered me across the room to a couple sitting on a velvet settee and chatting quietly. "J.B., let me introduce you to my counterpart at the *World*. This is Sam Stackhouse, reporter and new resident in Tulsa. And Sam, this lovely lady is Mrs. Stradford," said Smitherman, bowing slightly to Augusta.

Augusta Stradford smiled softly and responded, "I'm pleased to meet you Mr. Stackhouse. You will find these gentlemen to be scoundrels, so mind that you don't take them too seriously."

I laughed at her comment and said, "And you, Mrs. Stradford, must not take them too seriously either. I most definitely am not Mr. Smitherman's counterpart. I am a lowly reporter and am honored to be in the company of such men as your husband and Mr. Smitherman. I am afraid I was eavesdropping and heard that you enjoy the theater. May I ask what are your favorite plays?"

"Why yes, Mr. Stackhouse. I do so love the opportunity we have in the summers to go back to the city and take in a play or two. My favorites are usually Shakespearean dramas. I must say I enjoy the wicked Lady Macbeth a bit too much," said Mrs. Stradford.

"Ah, I do agree. Till Birnam Wood do come to Dunsinane, I shall agree!"

Mrs. Stradford laughed and said, "A.J. I do believe you have finally brought a guest here who actually has good taste!"

The men accepted the criticism with a slight chuckle and admitted they had difficulty sitting through these performances their wives adored.

We were pleasantly interrupted by Mrs. Smitherman's announcing, "Ladies and gentlemen, dinner is about to be served, so if you will take your places around the table, we can enjoy our meal and pleasant conversation." We all took our cue and found a chair in front of an inscribed place card with our name on it. Mrs. Smitherman sat at one end of the table and A. J. at the other. I was situated between Mr. Gurley and Doctor Jackson. Soon white-gloved waiters brought in steaming trays of roasted quail and succulent garden vegetables followed by linen-covered baskets filled with hot bread. I don't think I had ever experienced anything quite like that dinner. The chandelier above us was dimmed so that its lights twinkled off the droplets of crystal. The conversation was tame but interesting. It gave no clue of what would follow when the men retired to the library while the ladies chatted in the parlor.

The ladies took their cue when Mr. Smitherman rose and offered a toast to his guests. He nodded to his wife and she to the ladies, who smiled and dabbed their lips with linen napkins. I had no idea what was to follow. I had been quite at ease in dining salon, but now the air seemed to stiffen around me.

"Gentlemen," Smitherman said, "If you will follow me, we will allow the ladies leave of our presence so they might discuss us—hopefully with great favor." Everyone chuckled, and the ladies mocked his gesture with their own. A bevy of silk shirts rustled into the parlor. The men stood, and each bowed slightly to his wife as she exited. The rich swaths of silk made quite an impression on me as they departed, almost silently, like a spring rainbow moving toward the horizon.

Johnson circulated through the room offering each of us a fresh glass of wine as we followed our host into his library. Sturdy leather chairs focused on the vast fireplace that anchored the room. I took one of the chairs on the perimeter, wishing to observe rather than be observed, but Smitherman had other ideas. "Oh come now, Mr. Stackhouse. Take this chair. We are ever so interested in your opinions."

His sugar-sweet tone reminded me of my fourth grade teacher, the one who hated me.

"Oh, I couldn't do that, Mr. Smitherman. You have far worthier guests than I to share that honor. I'll just float along with the tide and watch."

"I insist. Please be my guest host. We have some rather important matters to discuss, and I am certain we should all like to hear your thoughts." There was no getting out of this mess. I could no longer gauge Smitherman's demeanor. I was trapped between stone and leather.

Each man took his seat. Some lit cigars passed around by the ever present Johnson. Striking a match on the nearest stone of the fireplace, Smitherman puffed gently on his cigar, and it came to life. The others followed suit. I held mine in my frozen hand, un-lit. Walking alone on the streets of Harlem at midnight was never as intimidating as this room had become.

Smitherman began, "Sam, I understand you covered the lynching of Roy Belton for the *World*. Is that correct?"

I looked askance at him and answered, "Yes."

"And how did you feel about that event? No journalistic answers, just gut feelings."

"Ill, physically ill," I responded honestly.

"So you did not approve of Belton's lynching? You do know he was of low character, don't you? And he was most certainly guilty," Smitherman argued.

I rose to leave the room, but Smitherman smiled and put his hand on my shoulder. "Sit down Sam. I merely wanted to rattle your cage a bit. A man needs to know the metal of his associates—and his adversaries."

I duly noted that he did not say *friends*, but rather *associates*. I clearly was not in the former category, and I was beginning to wonder if he considered me an adversary. I wondered if I had been lured into some sick game of cat and mouse. I was the lone white face not only in the room, but in the entire town at this time of night. I hesitated, but Smitherman motioned for me to sit. His face was neither one of approval nor disapproval. Nevertheless, I sat in the designated chair—or hot seat as I assumed it might be.

"As most of you know, Sam is a journalist. As far as I can tell, he is a reasonably unbiased one at that. His articles about the recent lynching in Tulsa indicated to me that he favors the rule of law rather than rule by mob. Is that accurate, Sam?" Smitherman asked.

"Yes," I answered cautiously. "I interviewed Belton. I was

aware of his character, if you want to call it that. He disgusted me, but he was still a man and a legal citizen of this country. As such he was entitled to protection under United States law. He should have been hung, but not by a vigilante mob."

"And how did you perceive local law enforcement's participation in the event?" Smitherman asked.

"I think you know the answer to that question." I answered.

Smitherman laughed but the others sat puzzled by this exchange.

"Yes, I'm quite sure I do. Sam, my people weren't invited to this celebrated event. I guess you could say we were kept in the dark," Smitherman said.

Johnson circulated with a chilled bottle to fill our glasses. I smiled at him, and he filled mine. I settled back into my chair as did the rest of the guests.

"Sam, we would appreciate your honest and full account of what happened that night, the account you could not publish. Are you willing to tell us about it?" Smitherman asked. At least he gave me the option of remaining silent.

"What do you want to know? And more importantly, why do you want to know?" I asked.

"Do you think it irrelevant to us?" Smitherman asked.

"Yes, I suppose I do," I replied. "Belton was white and as guilty as sin."

"Sam, if the white citizens of Tulsa would do this to one of their own, what do you think will happen if a Negro man is accused of such crimes?" Smitherman asked, leaning forward toward me.

I stared at him for a minute then sighed deeply. I knew the answer. "A. J., Tulsa operates with a frontier mentality, you know that. Mobs are like bees in a hive when they are threatened. Once you shake the nest, they all come out stinging, and they will sting until they are exhausted or dead. I watched family men, men who took their wives to church on Sunday, as they became arms on a beast. They converged in a dark section of the road to Jenks and they strung him up. They used Nida's taxi as a platform to hang him. They cheered like fans at a rodeo as the taxi backed out and Belton strangled, jerking like a frog leg in a frying pan. The crowd cheered and drank as if it were a party. Then people got back in their cars and left him there."

"I must say, I'm only surprised by the fact that they left him there. Had he been one of us, the bees would not have been satisfied to leave him there. But I'm more interested in how the mob was able to take him from the jail. You know about that too, don't you Sam?"

I stared deeply into the fire and replied, "You know I do, don't you?"

"I know many things, Mr. Stackhouse. How did they free him from his cell? That I don't know," Smitherman asked.

"They simply came up the elevator, walked into the sheriff's office, and demanded the keys to the cell. He didn't help them, but he didn't interfere with them either. He made calls to ensure that they were not impeded. He provided 'traffic control' for the snake of cars."

"I figured as much. Gentlemen, we must not allow this to happen if a man of color is accused in this town. Lynchings are occurring all over the country. A mania is spreading like the plague. White men are trying to come to grips with our presence among them. They fear us, and for good reason. We have more strength than they because we have been forged with the fire of the whip and chains. We must be worthy adversaries and hold our own in this struggle. That is the only way we survive as a race of men. Many among us fought in the war and returned as heroes, but our lighter-skinned counterparts still do not see us as men. Some of our fathers were born into a chained world where men were sold as cattle and herded in even less propitious circumstances into worlds they could not control. We owe it to them to take back our dignity and protect our world today as best we can. We cannot allow one more act of violence and injustice to be perpetrated upon us. We must head off any potential threat by show of force and unity," Smitherman said.

He stood in front of the massive stone fireplace while the blaze lit his face with reflected fire, but it was the fire in his belly that heated the room. Two of the men raised their glasses to him and responded, "So right, A. J. What can we do?"

"We must be certain we have proper arms and are willing to use them. Most importantly, we must stand together against our enemies. We must be united and willing to take a stand. We shall stand in front of the Courthouse and guard any of our own who might be incarcerated because we know the law will not protect them. Our fine Sheriff Wooley is a joke. He can be bought, but he is not worth our dime. I say we stand against him and block him rather than paying him off if any problem should occur. Are you with me?" Smitherman asked.

O.W. Gurley spoke first in his soft deep voice, "Now A. J., I don't think it is all that dire. Surely we can find a peaceful way to protect Greenwood. We can stay out of the business of Tulsa's white community and leave them be. They don't come into Greenwood, for the most part. I think you may be over reacting a bit."

Dr. Jackson added, "I think O.W. is right. If we keep our young men out of mischief and teach them to keep clean faces, we will be safe. I see enough blood without adding to it. We will be safe if we mind our own business. There are plenty of good folks in Tulsa. They will stand up for us."

Smitherman stood and leaned against the heavy stone mantle. He answered, "A.C., I know you mean well, but we must be proactive if we want to protect our own. I'm working now to get Wooley thrown out. A new man is up for the job, and I've talked to him. His name is McCullough. He won't voluntarily turn a prisoner over to a mob as Wooley did, but he's just one man. We will have to help him if the need arises.

Man seeks to maintain a caste system. He looks for a man or a group to whom he can feel superior, and white men have used us to fill that role ever since they brought us here from Africa. Don't you see they sense our power and they fear us? We have more money, more land, and more power than the vast majority of Tulsa's white citizens. They see that more clearly every day. They will find a way to exert their perceived superiority. It is only a question of time. We must be ready for that day. We must be men and not slaves."

Dr. Jackson could smell the smoke of ruin in these words, so he shook his head and rubbed his chin saying, "A.J., I think we need to keep cool heads. We aren't slaves. We are men, but men with families and friends, so we need to be calm and not look for trouble. If we go looking, we will find it."

"A.C., you are a good man. You mean well, but you don't see clearly. Trouble will seek us out, and we must be ready when it does. That's all I'm saying," Smitherman replied.

I watched Smitherman haul these men into his boat. They would follow him into disaster, all except Dr. Jackson and O.W. Gurley. The irony is that Smitherman survived the holocaust but Dr. Jackson did not. He believed in the goodness of man right up to the moment the shotgun blast knocked him to the ground on his front lawn. He was unarmed with his hands in the air in front of his own home. He had never looked for trouble in his entire life, but it found him.

My assessment proved to be accurate. Over the next few months, Smitherman wrote frequent editorials in his newspaper, most of which went unnoticed by Tulsans on the other side of the tracks, but virtually all of Greenwood knew where Smitherman stood. They stood firmly in his shadow, a shadow that protected them with truth as he saw it. He ranted about the mania sweeping through the country regarding the Negro man's desire for white women, which I never quite understood, but even I knew

Smitherman was on target with this one. As is usually the case, men fear what they do not understand, and neither side of the tracks understood the other. An old South where white men frequently raped slave women whom they controlled assumed that if Negro men were to attain power and control, they would return the insult. Greenwood was quickly amassing money and power. Riots and lynchings were so prevalent as to go almost unnoticed during the turbulent years following World War I. And to add to the fire, Smitherman preached a doctrine of armed resistance. He belonged to the NAACP. He wanted the men of Greenwood to stand ready to protect their own, with guns and money, which ever was needed.

Smitherman's venom turned white Tulsa against him, but he was as concerned about the lynching of Roy Belton as he was about people of his own race who had been lynched. Tulsa police chief, Gustafson, had gone on record as saying he applauded the lynching of Roy Belton as a fine deterrent to crime. Conversely, Smitherman railed about the issue, saying, "There is no crime, however atrocious, that justifies mob violence." He considered lynchings to be a stain upon society. He asked for justice and fairness for all. He was a highly educated attorney, so it was clear to him that the lawlessness of 1920 was tearing society apart. He believed a man was innocent until proven guilty, but often he stood alone. His physical stature was not epic, but his spirit was. Unfortunately, an epic spirit sometimes brings about epic disaster. His statement that, "The lynching of Roy Belton explodes the theory that a prisoner is safe on the top of the courthouse from mob violence," although true, helped bring Greenwood to ruin. The destruction was made complete by inflammatory and untrue statements published in the *Tribune*, statements that rallied white Tulsa when Dick Rowland ran from an elevator on Memorial Day in 1921. The truth about Dick Rowland was not sensational and would not have made interesting headlines—hype and speculation did.

CHAPTER 6

TULSA TRIBUNE

The *Tulsa Tribune* was relatively new to Tulsa, having been started up only two years earlier. It was run by Richard Lloyd Jones who had worked as a magazine editor in New York, where sensationalism was the standard. Jones believed the road to success was paved with crisis, imagined or real. He never hesitated to stir the pot. He harped daily on the local crime issues and was constantly "investigating" wrong doing. He made sure local citizens knew that Tulsa had become a crime zone. What else could suck readers in more quickly than sordid details of a city in dire need of cleansing.

According to W.D. Williams who later taught at Booker T. Washington High School in Tulsa, the *Tulsa Tribune* published an article the day after Rowland was arrested titled "To Lynch Negro Tonight." Only ten days earlier, this same newspaper had published a lengthy front page article blaming relations between black men and white women for some of the city's crime problems, insisting that, "We've got to get to the hotels. We've got to kick out the Negro pimps if we want to stop this vice." They convinced Tulsans that the unstoppable crime wave was fueled by men from Greenwood who were trying to get rich off white vices. A church committee went into the high-crime neighborhoods and verified this, so readers assumed it must be true.

After an extended campaign against the local police, which cited their inability to combat crime, the *Tribune* ran a series of articles including, "Catch the Crooks," "Go After Them," "Promoters of Crime," "To Make Every Day Safe," "The City Failure," and "Make Tulsa Decent." These editorials were sensational and stirred the emotions of locals, who were led to believe that if they could get rid of Greenwood, they would get rid of crime in Tulsa.

By mid-May emotions were reaching a boiling point. An editorial on May 14, titled "Better Get Busy," warned officials that if they did not clean up the city, the citizens would. It spoke of an "awakened conscience" among citizens, a conscience that had been awakened by the *Tribune*. The *Tribune* had implicitly condoned the lynching of Roy Belton and had insisted that the city experienced a lull in crime after that lynching. They further insisted that African American men were at the root of the city's problems since they were the ones who provided the whores for the prostitution trade and were known to provide illegal alcohol to speakeasy customers. The paper described clubs where white girls danced to the music of Negro piano players in a world where men and women of different races were strictly forbidden to mingle. They insisted that Negro men were behind all this misbehavior.

Then to finish off this slide to disaster, on May 26 twelve prisoners escaped from the jail on the fourth floor of the new courthouse. This was disturbing to citizens who were already fearful of local crime, then on May 30, six more prisoners escaped. The prisoners sawed through poorly constructed bars on windows and doors and shimmied down the four-story drop on bed sheets tied together.

This was the milieu into which Dick Rowland and Sarah

Page stepped on May 31. The *Tribune* had whipped its readers into a frenzy pitch. The *Star* had whipped its readers into a similar frenzy, insisting they must be proactive with a show of arms and force should any Greenwood man be arrested. The populace of Tulsa had been led to believe that lynching was a perfectly acceptable alternative to a drawn out and potentially useless legal process carried out by inept law enforcement. Now this community was fearful of criminals escaping from its new jail. This scenario was bound to end in tragedy. It was a short leap to the conclusion that a Greenwood man accused of raping a white woman should be quickly lynched. Considering the seething envy of the wealth of some of Greenwood's residents, the outcome was inevitable.

CHAPTER 7

DICK ROWLAND AND SARAH PAGE

Dick Rowland and Sarah Page had known each other for quite some time. Both were orphans and had struggled to survive. Struggle often forms bonds. No one is quite certain how tight the bond was between these two young people (some insist they were lovers—others say definitely not), but their fates came together on May 30, 1921. Dick, who was 19 years old, worked shining shoes in a shop near the Drexel Building on Main Street in Tulsa. Since he was not allowed to use white restrooms and had to work long hours, he was allowed to use the restroom at the top of the Drexel Building, but to get there, he had to ride up in the elevator. The elevator was run by Sarah Page, who was paying her way through secretarial school with her wages. Dick was not supposed to work that day, but for some unknown reason he was on duty even though the town was mostly empty.

Dick looked around and saw no potential customers, so he laid his rag carefully across his brushes and started across the street to the Drexel Building. The sun was bright. He shielded his eyes with his hand. He looked down the usually busy street and saw no cars. He knew business would not be good that day, but he had hoped to pick up a little extra money. He opened the door and stepped into the shadow of the building. Sarah smiled at him. He returned the smile a bit awkwardly. "Morning, Miss Sarah," Dick said.

He looked down at the marble floor and walked across the distance between them. He was happy to be inside out of the sun, and seeing Sarah working today was a pleasant surprise. She smiled as she watched him approaching her elevator. "I saw you were working and wondered if I would get to see you today," she said.

"Yes ma'am. I'm working. I thought more folks would be in town, but looks like I won't make my dime today," Dick replied as he approached her.

Sarah had heard about Dick's football honors and noticed how muscular he was. She liked him. He was always friendly and respectful. She stood just inside the elevator with the door open and waited for him. He stepped inside. As she began to close the door, the elevator suddenly lurched. She fell toward Dick. She screamed. He caught her in his arms. When she looked up at him, he panicked. He let her go and ran from the elevator and the Drexel Building as fast as his feet would carry him, not even stopping to collect his gear at the shoe shine stand.

The lone clerk working that day in Renberg's clothing store next door had watched Dick cross the street. He mistrusted anyone from Greenwood and didn't like having Dick around when the streets were nearly empty. He wondered what he might be up to going into the Drexel Building. When he heard Sarah scream and saw Dick dash out the door and disappear behind the building, he assumed the boy had harmed Sarah. He picked up the phone and called the Tulsa police then ran toward the door of the Drexel Building. He quickly reached Sarah, who was standing in the corner of the elevator crying. The clerk took her hand and led her out to a chair. She was sitting there crying when the police arrived minutes later.

Sarah insisted, "Leave me be. I'm alright. I just fell." No one believed her.

The police put her into their car and took her to the station. They interrogated her for the rest of the afternoon and into the evening. They kept asking the same questions, but she kept insisting she had fallen when the elevator malfunctioned. She had no wounds indicating she had fallen, so they were insistent that something else had happened. Some investigators speculated that she was embarrassed to tell the truth. Others whispered that she was known to be a loose woman, so she might have been flirting with the shine boy. She had a reputation. She was a single woman with no family. She lived on her own. They hinted at how she supported herself.

Sarah was uninjured and her clothes unruffled, but the police decided it was attempted rape. Sarah, however, refused to sign a statement to that effect. The police finally released her late that night, but she could hear whispers from two of the officers as she was leaving. They pointed at her and snickered. She recognized one of them.

Rumors of Sarah's reputation seeped out through the community. Sarah had been on her own for most of her growing-up years, so voices were quick to speculate. Prostitution was a thriving business in Tulsa, so some wanted to accuse a girl who had no one to defend her except a boy from Greenwood, who would lose his life if he did. She told the truth, but others preferred hype. Hype won out.

Rowland ran for home and Miss Damie, the only person would defend him. He waited. He knew police would come. He was a shy young man terrified of what might happen to him. The next morning, the police came. Tulsa police officers, Detective Henry Carmichael and Patrolman Henry C. Pack, took Rowland into custody.

The officers knocked on Damie Ford's front door. She

opened the door and stared at them. She knew Henry Pack. She looked directly into his eyes with steely determination. "You ain't gonna hurt my boy. I ain't gonna let you, you know that don't you, Henry?"

"Yes, ma'am. I do. I'm just doing my job, Miss Damie. You know that too," Henry answered. Henry was a big man, but gentle. "I'm sorry, Miss Damie," he added. He, too, feared for Dick's life.

"Dick, come on out here," Damie called out.

Dick appeared in the doorway, trembling. His shoulders slumped and his head down, he stood beside his adopted mother.

"You gotta come down to the station, Dick. Go peaceable and we'll look after you best we can," Pack said. Damie Ford glared and her nostrils flared, but she kept quiet, at least until they were gone.

Dick looked back at Damie with tears in his eyes as he went out the door. He doubted he would ever see her again. She was the closest thing he had to family. He trembled visibly as he stumbled down the steps to the waiting police car. Pack opened the door and told him to get in. Dick looked back at Miss Damie once more as the car pulled away from the house.

They took him first to the police station then later to the courthouse. He was interrogated for hours at the police station. He insisted all the while that nothing had happened and he had not tried to harm Sarah. The same officers who had snickered at Sarah watched with disgust. They wanted retribution, not truth. They were sick of being accused of doing nothing to stem the tide of crime in Tulsa.

Patrolman Pack was one of only a few African American officers on the seventy-five-man police force. He assisted when they moved Dick from the police station to the jail at the top of the courthouse. Pack held Dick's handcuffed arms while he walked him up the steps to the courthouse, but his last gesture before turning him over to the sheriff was a pat on the back and a single comment: "Good luck, buddy." Pack knew what would happen next.

The warmth of Pack's hand on Dick's back remained with him when they shoved him into a cell. Dick sat down in the dark cell on a stiff cot and looked around him. He felt once again like the six-year-old child abandoned on the street by parents who could not take care of him. The only difference was that now Damie Ford would not be able to help him.

Damie Ford, who had taken that frightened six-year-old child under her wing and nurtured him, immediately hired a lawyer to represent him. She knew as well as he did what could and probably would happen to him. She knew the truth about what had happened in the Drexel Building, but that would not help Dick. No one was likely to believe him or her. They would believe the hype. They would believe what they wanted to believe.

By the time the *Tribune* went to press on May 31st, Rowland was locked in a cell in the courthouse and peering hopelessly between iron bars. The paper went to work doing its job. That afternoon a boy stood on the street in downtown Tulsa waving copies of the *Tribune* and shouting, "A Negro assaults a white girl!" Tulsans came out of shops along the street to grab their copy of the news. Talk of a lynching began immediately. Truth no longer mattered. Rowland had been tried and convicted by the press.

I tried to interview Rowland, but was turned away by deputies guarding him. Elevators in the courthouse were disabled. The same stairs I had used to witness the taking of Roy Belton from his cell, were now heavily guarded. I approached the stairwell cautiously, but when I opened the door, I was met by a large man wearing a khaki uniform and a badge. He held a ten-gauge shotgun at his side.

The deputy said, "Buddy, you need to mind your own business. No one sees the prisoner." He was calm and not overtly threatening, but I got the message.

I said, "I'm from the *World*, here to interview Rowland."

"Sorry. No one sees the prisoner. Now leave the building," the deputy said firmly. I left. I couldn't interview him and neither had the *Tribune*, but guilty he was by order of the press. The *Tribune* sold out of papers. An "informed" public began to move.

A crowd began to gather in front of the courthouse at Sixth and Boulder. Stetsons in motorcars arrived in masses. Traffic stacked up and men, women, and children rushed on foot to join the angry hive. They shouted racial slurs and demands for justice. By sunset they numbered in the hundreds. By 7:30 they were shouting in organized chants, "Let us have the nigger!"

The crowd jeered and taunted the Sheriff and his men. They wanted Sheriff Wooley's brand of justice, but McCullough had other ideas. He would not repeat the actions of his predecessor. He disabled the elevators as soon as he had Rowland in custody, and he immediately stationed six of his men armed with rifles and shotguns on the roof of the stone courthouse. Other deputies barricaded the stairwells with orders to shoot intruders.

McCullough appeared on the steps of the courthouse with a bullhorn and attempted to reason with the crowd. He shouted, "Go home and leave the law to do its job. The law will take care of this matter. I will not allow anyone to enter the courthouse. Now disperse!"

One Stetson shouted, "Just like you let those prisoners escape last week? You better get out of the way, or we'll take you down too!"

The crowd began to advance on the Sheriff, so two deputies standing beside him raised their shotguns. The crowd stopped advancing, but the jeering continued. McCullough went back inside, and the deputies backed slowly toward the courthouse with their weapons still trained on the crowd. Snipers on the roof made their presence more noticeable, and soon the doors slammed and were bolted shut.

At 8:20 three men tried to enter the courthouse. A visibly

angry Sheriff McCullough turned them away. I was too far away to hear what was said, but it was obviously a tense scene. The men were enraged, and I knew nothing good would come of this. Needless to say, the white mob was not happy and left only to re-group and add numbers to their thousand-headed beast.

News of the attempted kidnap of Rowland flew through Greenwood. Willie Williams heard the news and hurried over to his family business, the Dreamland Theater. The Dreamland was owned by Willie's parents, John and Loula Williams who also owned the Williams Building at the corner of Greenwood Avenue and Archer Street. The theater was a 750-seat theater that offered live musical and theatrical revues as well as silent movies accompanied by a piano player. The theater was in a state of confusion and panic. A man in the theater jumped up onto the stage and shouted, "We're not going to let this happen. We are going to go downtown and stop this lynching. Close this place down." And they did. Twenty-four hours later, the beautiful theater would be a burned-out shell with its sign hanging from one remaining chain. It was the culmination of a lifetime of work for the Williams family.

Dreamland Theater

The same reaction was happening all across Greenwood. It was a community under siege, and the most vocal of the concerned citizens was A.J. Smitherman.

Prior to this time, the only lynchings in or near Tulsa had been white men, but Smitherman knew that was almost certain to be the fate of Dick Rowland. This was the very situation he had repeatedly warned his readers about. He quickly gathered supporters and held a critical conference. He stirred them to action, insisting they resist with arms if necessary. They must be willing to lay down their lives to protect Rowland and Greenwood. Two years earlier, these same men had thwarted a threatened lynching of another Greenwood resident by a strong show of force, and they were determined to achieve the same outcome for Rowland. Among his supporters were J. B. Stradford and Dr. Bridgewater, who had led armed men downtown to rescue three young men in the previous protest. They were quite vocal about their cause and were joined by more than a few armed veterans, who had recently fought for liberty for all Americans. These same veterans must now fight for their own survival. Once again they were ready to lay down their lives to protect one of their own. Their lives and homes were in far more danger than anyone except Smitherman suspected.

O. W. Gurley and Barney Cleaver, a deputy sheriff and a resident of Greenwood, argued against this plan, fearing the worst. Cleaver told the group, "Sheriff McCullough is a good man, not like Wooley. He will protect Dick. We need to let the law handle this. If you go down to the courthouse, there is sure to be bloodshed." Cleaver tried to stay in contact with Sheriff McCullough to assure the gathering crowd that Rowland was safe, but to no avail. The men ignored his warnings and listened to Smitherman.

Smitherman told the men, "Come on boys, let's go downtown!" They followed the piper into disaster.

Around 9:00 pm the night of May 31, approximately 25 men from Greenwood cast their lot. They left Greenwood in a caravan of automobiles. They formed a somber and determined militia armed with shotguns, handguns, and rifles. They parked their cars in front of the courthouse and got out with their weapons visible. Darkness obscured their faces, but I could see they meant business. To a man, they stood tall and kept their hands on their weapons. The more diminutive Smitherman stood at the front of the group. The sheriff came down the steps and met with the group. The body language was different from the earlier confrontation on the steps. McCullough understood the men's concern, but I could see he was trying to get them to leave. I inched closer and heard him say, "Rowland is safe. My men will guard him. No one will hand him over to a mob. I assure you of that! Do you see those men on the roof? They are crack shots, and they have orders to kill anyone who attempts to take him. Now you must go home. If you persist, you will bring ruin on the entire community. Now go!"

Smitherman waved his shotgun in the air and motioned for the rest of the men to return to their cars. Standing on the top step, he looked around carefully. Finally he went back to his car and started the engine. He turned his car around, and the rest followed. Unfortunately, I was not the only one to witness this event, and news travels fast in situations like this.

No movement goes unnoticed in a tense environment, and a mob of another color that had been forming earlier picked up steam and soon was 1,000 strong. The tall man with the Stetson hat stood at the head of this beast as he had the last one. The men were shocked that armed men from Greenwood had come to the jail. They would not stand for such protest. They began to gather men and weapons for an all out siege of the jail since they had realized the new sheriff would not be quite as accommodating as Wooley had been. The Stetson could not simply grab the prisoner from his cell this time.

Sheriff McCullough looked out his office window at the street below and knew he would have difficulty fending off the mass of angry men determined to have their own brand of justice, but he was not going to allow mob rule. He was sworn to uphold the law, and he would lay down his life before he would violate that oath.

Meanwhile at the local National Guard Armory, Major James Bell was put on alert. He didn't think real problems would arise, but he was prepared to protect his men and weapons. He quietly called his men to duty. When the men started to arrive, they found three or four hundred men pulling at the window gratings, trying to enter the armory to steal weapons and ammunition. The guardsmen quickly took their positions and stood together to defend the armory. The marauders were successfully repelled, but they left with threats. The guardsmen told the mob they had weapons sufficient only for themselves and those weapons were government property. They steadfastly refused to hand any weapons or ammunition over to the mob. They were prepared to shoot unauthorized intruders. Apparently the men believed them, so they turned their efforts elsewhere.

By this time, the mob outside the courthouse had grown to more than 2,000 men, women, and children. Several local leaders, including Reverend Charles Kerr of the First Presbyterian Church and a local judge, tried unsuccessfully to persuade the mob to return to their homes and let law enforcement handle the matter, but to no avail. Oddly enough, local police were not present in any significant numbers. Only five policemen were on duty between the courthouse and Brady hotel at the time. These were the same men who directed traffic to the lynching of Roy Belton.

At 10:00 pm when the Greenwood men made their second attempt to protect Rowland and the riot began, Police Chief Gustafson was not "interfering with the will of the people," but instead was sitting in his office at police headquarters.

Too many opposing forces were about to clash: the *Tribune* was clearly fanning the fire and gathering the mob, the local police were staying out of the way and allowing the sore to fester, Smitherman was gathering his troops again and insisting on a second armed response to any attempt to take Rowland, and the white mob at the courthouse was growing and becoming more restive with every hour that passed. Each of these forces had reasons for its stance, but it is highly unlikely that any of the instigators actually knew Rowland and either sought to lynch him or come to his defense because of their knowledge of him or his alleged offense. None of them actually knew the truth, and few cared about the truth at all. One side wanted to destroy Greenwood. The other side wanted to protect it. It was much more about Greenwood than about Rowland. Rowland was an excuse. Meanwhile Rowland shivered in his cell and listened in horror to the gathering crowds.

Nervous citizens of Greenwood also shivered. Church and community groups dispersed early. Parents and grandparents kept their families inside. Still, a large group of concerned citizens was gathering outside the *Star*.

Smitherman, who did not know Rowland, was the lynchpin for the Greenwood community, keeping them informed of events as they occurred, but he had a larger agenda. He felt a calling to protect African Americans who were abused by a post-Civil War mentality and were often in need of an advocate. As a charter member of the NAACP, he knew the dangers they faced. He had the pulpit and the financial and intellectual capital to carry out measures he deemed necessary, which he continued to do as long as he lived, even after the Greenwood he knew had ceased to exist. Smitherman made sure Greenwood residents realized the gravity of the situation. Some of the residents knew Dick Rowland, so their agenda was simply to save one of their own. For this, some lost their lives and almost all lost their homes and livelihood, as did

Smitherman. Although Rowland was shy and quiet, he had played football for the Greenwood High School and was well liked by his neighbors. He was always willing to lend a helping hand when he could since he had been forced to accept the help of strangers when he was a child. Consequently, the citizens of Greenwood gathered to offer the help he needed to survive. None of them believed he could be guilty of rape. It simply did not fit the young man they knew.

As Greenwood residents grew more anxious, a few cars at a time began to make their way back into town to learn what they could of the unfolding crisis and to show white mobs they would not go down without a fight. The cars leaving Greenwood had visible firearms and determined drivers. Unfortunately, the message they were trying to send was mistaken for an all out uprising and soon turned to disaster.

CHAPTER 8

THE RIOT

Whether the white mob tried to storm the courthouse or whether they only waited for the right opportunity to snatch Rowland, I'm not sure. They appeared extremely menacing to me as they must have to the Greenwood men. The mob's numbers continued to increase, and shouts were getting louder by the minute. They shouted threats and slurs and waved weapons at the sentinels on the roof as the night wore on. To say they were threatening Rowland's safety would be an understatement. In any case, the caravan from Greenwood made a second attempt to defend Rowland from the swarming hive. The men drove to the courthouse, got out of their cars at Sixth and Main, and marched single-file to the courthouse steps right through the swarm of people. Smitherman walked up to the door being guarded by a deputy and waited to speak to the sheriff. He repeated the offer to help defend Rowland, and again the offer was refused. He walked back to his group of men and told them they would have to return to Greenwood.

The group intended to leave peacefully, but as they were

leaving the courthouse the second time, the Stetson approached a tall World War I veteran, who was carrying his Army-issue hand gun. "Nigger," he said, "What are you doing with that pistol?"

The veteran declared, "I'm going to use it if I need to."

The Stetson demanded, "No, you give it to me!"

The veteran's response: "Like hell I will!" He had used this weapon to defend the very man who now demanded he relinquish it, and he was not about to surrender his rights. When the Stetson attempted to take the gun from the veteran, a shot was fired. The riot began. I watched from the fringes of the crowd, but I could never be sure whether the shot was accidental or intentional. I am not even sure whether it was the tall soldier who fired the shot, but it didn't matter after that.

The white mob opened fire on the retreating Greenwood men. They took cover as best they could and returned fire. Men scrambled to reach their cars, jumping over bushes and park benches as they fled. I ducked behind the corner of the courthouse and didn't see who was firing. The initial volley lasted only a few seconds, but when it ended as many as a dozen men lay dead or wounded on the street in front of the courthouse. The Greenwood men were outnumbered twenty to one. Those who could, retreated to Greenwood with the white mob firing at them as they went. Heavy gunfire was heard along Fourth Street as the men fled. I ran toward Greenwood, following the fleeing cars and trying to dodge gunfire.

I came upon Dr. George Miller, who heard the gunfire and came outside to see if he could help a man who had been shot. He was gaping at the mayhem on the street when I reached him. He seemed to be frozen in a trance as he stared at the man's body lying in the street in front of his office. The shooter kept running, chasing other men, but another group stopped. Several of the men stabbed the bleeding man before running off to find other victims. The man's blood pooled in the street beneath his head, then he was still. His shirt and trousers were torn where first bullets then knives had penetrated.

Miller said, "I saw the man writhing in pain in the street, and I came out to see if I could help him, but more men came along and shoved me out of the way. They stabbed him repeatedly and rushed off to follow the others. What in heaven's name is happening? I wanted to help him, but more angry men were gathering around him even after I could see he was dead. They refused to allow the driver of the ambulance, which had just arrived to pick him up." Miller was clearly bewildered.

Miller continued, "It is an impossible situation. I could be of no help. The crowd is getting more and more belligerent. The Negro had been shot so many times, and onlookers were slashing him with knives." Miller, still in a daze, turned away from me and got in his car and drove away. This was just the beginning. It was the darkest day any of us had ever known. I could never have guessed that by dawn it would be even worse.

Soon another skirmish broke out at Second and Cincinnati. Now the men from Greenwood were fighting for their own lives, not the life of Dick Rowland. Rowland was safely under the protection of Sheriff McCullough, but the rest of Greenwood was on its own against the killer bees. The Greenwood men fled across the Frisco tracks to their homes, where they thought they would be safe. I passed more than a dozen of them either dead or dying along the way. They had been unable to get back to their cars and had fled on foot with the white mob behind them. Gunshots rang out all around me, and the air smelled of smoke and fear. The heat of the night had turned into an inferno of its own. Men began to act out suppressed envy and hatred as they became one beast emboldened by anonymity. They were no longer individual men with a conscience, but an abstract entity free from ethical restrictions.

Hoping law enforcement was coming to the rescue, I ran back toward the courthouse, but no one was rushing to aid the Greenwood residents. Rowland was under heavy guard, but throngs of angry Tulsans were still loitering in dark shadows about the jail, many holding rifles or shotguns in one hand and a liquor bottle in the other. Some had pistols stuck in their belts as well. It almost seemed a celebratory event. Bursts of laughter could be heard occasionally as they talked. I could only guess at the reason for the laughter. They were finally getting what they wanted: retribution against the "niggers with money," whom they so vehemently envied. From time to time groups of men would return from skirmishes and report on their exploits to the delight of the crowd. Groups clustered and planned what to do next. They worked out strategies to get into Greenwood and wreak more havoc.

Just a few blocks away, the police chief, the same one who had ordered his men to direct traffic when Roy Belton was lynched, was deputizing a mob of nearly 500 men and boys as "Special Deputies." Some were given badges, and when those ran out, the rest were handed ribbons, but either was treasured as a status symbol. They were now small men with big power. They were sworn to uphold the law. But whose law were they intending to enforce? I soon had my answer. They stormed down the street toward Greenwood with their chests puffed out and their rifles locked and loaded.

The ones who didn't have weapons soon acquired them. A uniformed police officer shouted, "Get a gun and get a nigger!" And they did. They began breaking into nearby sporting goods stores, pawn shops, and hardware stores and taking weapons and ammunition at will. First Dick Bardon's store on First Street was hit. They smashed the glass in the door and unlocked it then flooded in. It was a mad rush to get the best guns. It was like Christmas come early for men who had never had enough money to buy weapons they wanted. Now they could take what they wanted, and no one would ever know who they were. Next they smashed in the window at J.W. McGee's Sporting Goods shop on Second Street—directly across the street from the Police station.

The chief stood in the doorway across the street and laughed as the marauders plundered McGee's life's work. McGee could only stand and watch while a Tulsa Police officer handed out guns and ammunition snatched from his inventory. The men pretended to be "borrowing" the weapons. Some he knew; some he didn't. McGee knew he would never see any of the guns again. He may not have opposed the riot in general, but he certainly opposed his loss of inventory. He had no intention of arming the militia at his own expense.

William Holway, an engineer in Tulsa, told me the next day that he was at the Rialto Theater when someone ran into the theater and shouted, "Nigger fight, nigger fight!" and the theater emptied. He said he took cover behind a pillar in front of Younkman's drug store and watched as a Greenwood man ran across the alley, and someone cut him down with a shotgun blast. The man lay there writhing in pain but Holway didn't dare move to try to help him. Mass insanity had taken over. The best he could do was take cover. Only when the action moved farther toward Greenwood did he come out from his hiding place and inch toward his home, but still he could hear the sound of distant gunfire and smell smoke all around him.

According to William "Choc" Phillips, who later became a Tulsa police officer, in another theater nearby, a similar drama was occurring. He said the mob was chasing a Greenwood man behind the theater when the man saw the stage door. He ducked inside and was trying to hide in the cover of darkness when suddenly he found himself on stage and blinded by the light. He dashed for the orchestra pit where he was cut down by white men who had followed him through the stage door. Chaos ruled. Gunfire spattered the audience. Casualties included whites and blacks as random shots fired in confusion caught many who were simply in the wrong place at the wrong time. Couples who had been quietly watching the show were cowering under their seats in terror. They had not even been aware of the riot, but now they were caught in the crossfire.

The chaos elsewhere also took victims of both races. One white Tulsan was killed in his car in a case of mistaken identity. Others died as random gunfire caught confused bystanders gaping at the melee. Many were so taken by surprise they could not find cover fast enough.

Around midnight, another crowd began to gather at the courthouse shouting, "Bring the rope" and "Get the nigger," but they were less interested in Rowland than the issue in general. They saw an opportunity to bring down Greenwood, which they saw as the root of all their problems. Sporadic gunfire could be heard all night as pockets of fighting occurred, the heaviest of which was across the Frisco yards.

Passengers on an incoming train were forced to take cover as gunfire sprayed their train. A few carloads of whites ventured into Greenwood to fire randomly into homes and businesses. Two particularly tragic victims of this gunfire were an elderly couple saying their evening prayers before going to bed. They lived in a modest home in Greenwood and were harming no one. A mob broke into the house and shot them in the back of the head, splattering their brains over their bed as they prayed. The mob then pillaged their home and set it afire. It was one of the first fires set.

Once the mobs began to burn houses, the Tulsa fire department was forced away by rioters holding them at gunpoint. The mob refused to allow the helpless firemen to put out the flames. By 4:00 am, more than two dozen businesses in Greenwood had been burned to the ground, the Dreamland Theater among them.

Sheriff McCullough requested assistance from the local National Guard around 9:30 pm when the trouble began, but it took them more than an hour to arrive. By then the trouble was well underway and was out of control.

The arrival of the National Guard did not help to quell the riot. These National Guardsmen were exclusively white and did not play an impartial role in the keeping of order. Many of them saw the situation as a "Negro uprising," and referred to the Greenwood men as "the enemy."

The Tulsa police armed the National Guardsmen with a machine gun, which they mounted on the back of a truck. This was supposed to help the Guard "maintain order." The machine gun, however, was in poor condition and could only fire one shell at a time.

An area on Detroit Avenue between Brady Street and Standpipe Hill marked an invisible boundary between black and white areas, so about thirty Guardsmen stationed themselves along that line. Guardsmen rounded up some of the Greenwood men in the immediate area and handed them over to the police. They were taken to holding areas under the guise of protective custody.

Rounding up Greenwood residents

Word reached Greenwood that they were being invaded by white mobs, so many of them armed themselves and took positions to defend their homes. They loaded their own weapons and stood at windows and doors waiting or on rooftops watching. They mistakenly believed they could defend their homes.

Others streamed out of Greenwood in a frantic exodus, hoping to find shelter out of harm's way. Some were successful, but others were not. Billy Hudson, who lived on Archer, hitched up his wagon and attempted to take his grandchildren to safety. Gunmen cut him down along the way.

Another strategy some took was that of surrendering peacefully to authorities, who were roaming about rounding up Greenwood residents. Some believed the guardsmen were there to insure their safety and followed them willingly, and to be fair, some of them were taken to safety outside the riot area. Others were not so fortunate.

Dr. A.C. Jackson was one of the unfortunate. When the mob reached Dr. Jackson's home, he came out the door with his hands up. Dr. Jackson was a renowned surgeon, said by the Mayo Clinic to be the best Negro surgeon in the country. He was a gentle man dedicated to helping others. He had an elegant home on North Detroit, along the shoulder of Standpipe Hill. He came out saying, "Here I am boys, don't shoot." Witnesses say it was between 7:30 and 8:00 the morning of June 1. One man shot him twice, then when he was down, another shot him in the leg and broke it. They left him lying there to die then burned his home to the ground after taking what they wanted from the home.

Rumors ran rampant through both black and white crowds. One particularly destructive rumor declared that a train load (500 armed men) was due to arrive at the Midland Valley Railway passenger station off Third Street. A National Guard patrol rushed to the depot and found there was no such train. Thirty minutes later the guardsmen heard that black gunmen were firing on white residences on Sunset Hill north of Standpipe Hill. They heard a white woman had been shot, so they deployed their defective machine gun to mow down the resistance.

So many white Tulsans rushed to join the melee that streets

became clogged and men had to abandon their cars and start running toward Greenwood. Rather than having police officers try to maintain order, Chief Gustafson ordered them to guard roads into the city and protect the city water works along Sand Springs Road. One-fifth of the officers on duty were assigned to protect the ice plant near the Eleventh Street Bridge.

Local National Guard officers could see they needed help so Major Byron Kirkpatrick attempted to summon assistance. He contacted Adjutant General Charles F. Barrett, who then spoke with Governor Robertson. Robertson instructed him to obtain the signed request as required by law to activate the National Guard for a civil crisis. This request had to be signed by the chief of police, the county sheriff, and a local judge. Unfortunately, the sheriff was barricaded in the jail atop the courthouse, and no one could get to him to have him sign the paper.

Greenwood burning

More than three hours lapsed before this petition could be obtained and transmitted to the governor. This time lapse was critical. The telegram finally arrived at the Governor's office at 1:46 am. It read: "Governor J.B.A. Robertson Oklahoma City, Oklahoma. Race riot developed here. Several killed. Unable handle situation. Request that National Guard forces be sent by special train. Situation serious."

At 2:15 am Major Kirkpatrick learned that the governor had authorized troops to be sent to Tulsa and that they would arrive on a special train leaving Oklahoma City at 5:00 am. Precious time was passing. People were being slaughtered and houses burned. The holocaust had begun. Greenwood was under all-out siege.

Just before dawn on June 1, thousands of armed white men gathered at the three railway stations, no longer concerned with Dick Rowland, but rather propelled by another force. They said they would end the riot, a riot that now involved chasing people who were hiding in their own homes. Ending the riot to them now involved burning the Greenwood homeland to the ground—completely annihilating it and sending its residents elsewhere, be that to the grave or another town. Before burning the homes and businesses, many of the men took whatever valuables they could find, including grand pianos and expensive furniture and jewelry as well as cash and weapons. They loaded trucks with loot before setting fire to the homes.

Burned out *Tulsa Star*

Smaller bands of men gathered at other areas and set about the same agenda. I watched five men in a green Franklin automobile pull up beside one of the groups and shout, "What the hell are you waitin' on? Let's go get 'em!" They sped off toward Deep Greenwood, the business section of town where I had met Gurley and Smitherman. Greenwood might not have been the aggressor, but neither were they hesitant to guard their homes and businesses. When the smoke cleared, I saw the green Franklin, stopped in the middle of Archer Street. It was riddled with bullet holes, and the bodies of the men inside were slumped against bloody leather seats. They got more than they planned for.

While these mobs were invading or preparing to invade Greenwood, many Greenwood residents were preparing to flee. Officers Pack and Lewis were encouraging residents to leave, saying that it would not be safe for them to remain in their homes. They were so right. No one was safe in Greenwood on June 1.

Mrs. Dimple Bush and her husband were staying at the Red Wing Hotel. When they heard that warning, she said, "We rushed out and found a taxi, which took us straight north on Greenwood." They managed to escape.

Julia Duff, a teacher at Booker T. Washington High School, where Dick Rowland had played football, was in her room when a friend came in and told her to get dressed because something was wrong. She peeked through the curtains and gasped when she saw soldiers all around, presumably the National Guardsmen. The soldiers were banging on doors and driving the men out of all the houses around them and onto Detroit Avenue. Confused and angry men stood in the street unaware of the real danger they were in. Those who resisted did not fare well. Noise and chaos filled the streets.

Duff's neighbor, Mr. Woods was running with his three-month-old baby in his arms. Three brutes were behind him with guns. Duff ducked back behind the curtain and never found out what happened to him.

So traumatized was Miss Duff that her legs gave way, and she had to crawl about the room, taking things from her closet and putting them into her trunk. She mistakenly thought the men would allow her to take her things with her if she packed them, but before she could finish packing, six men were at her door ordering the man of the house to come out with his hands up just as his neighbors had.

The pretense was to collect firearms from Greenwood houses. Perhaps at first the men only intended to collect the guns, but once they started, they became a herd of animals with animal instincts rather than human compassion. Torches came out, and the animal mentality spread with the frenzy.

A machine gun had been set up atop the grain elevator where throngs of angry men were gathering and waiting for daylight. Shortly before 5:00 am a siren sounded. As if on cue, the machine gun began to strafe nearby houses in Greenwood, and all hell broke loose. The masses gathered at the depots and other critical areas all began full assault on Greenwood at once. They poured across the Frisco tracks into Deep Greenwood. I never found out where that siren came from, but it was one of the most chilling sounds I have ever heard. I will remember it forever. The killer bees all seemed to know what it meant. They became one beast intent on destruction.

I ran toward the chaos and climbed atop a rail car to see what was happening. Suddenly men were crawling out of every nook and cranny like so many serpents loosed from a den. They had lurked in the dark and shadows waiting for the battle to begin. They burst to life with shrill battle cries. Some shrieked with rebel yells, some gobbled like Indians riding into battle, and some merely shouted. It was no longer a riot—it was a full invasion. Those who didn't participate in the mayhem were watching and encouraging, shouting and cheering the invaders on. It was nauseating. Smoke began to billow from Greenwood streets. I sat paralyzed for what seemed like an eternity. I could not comprehend what was before my eyes.

After guarding their homes and business during the long,

tense night, many Greenwood men had to retreat. John Wesley
Williams had kept watch over his apartment all night, but at dawn
bullets rained down on him, smashing windows and peppering the
walls. He ran for his life. He was able to squeeze off only a few
final rounds as he fled along the Midland Valley tracks, leaving his
home and business behind. He knew neither would be there when
and if he was able to return.

Others were experiencing the same fears. Mary E. Jones
Parrish and her daughter Florence Mary were so fearful they ran
out into Archer Street without taking time to get proper clothes.
The baby had no shoes or hat like many of their friends trying to
escape the melee. People were running about in their night clothes,
not knowing where to go to escape. Mary used her body to shield
her baby as they ran for their lives with the machine gun atop the
granary raining bullets all around them. Seeing women and
children screaming and running through the streets was something
I never thought I would see in this country.

Bullets were flying from windows where Greenwood men
had taken cover and were returning fire. Crossfire from advancing
white men chasing them caught anyone who came between them.

When Mary first ran into the street, it was mostly empty. Someone shouted at her, "Get out of the street with that child or you both will be killed!" In complete panic, she kept running. In the next block they were in the midst of the gunfight. They were hoping to get out of Greenwood and into the safety of a friend's home. They realized that to shelter in one of the buildings would mean sure death. By this time, it was apparent to them that Greenwood would be completely destroyed. Somehow they managed to reach safety but they never forgot the terror of June 1.

Many survivors remember seeing men, women, and children running and screaming in a futile effort to escape the holocaust around them. These were residents who had been peacefully sleeping and going about their lives in the quiet order of a safe community. When that whistle blew shortly after 5:00 am, their world changed forever. Life as they knew it would vanish in one day's time.

Not long after that whistle blew and the machine guns began firing, I saw several planes in the still-dim sky. They began flying over Greenwood and dropping incendiary devices on fleeing throngs. Some appeared to be sticks of dynamite. One man shouted, "Look out for the aeroplanes; they are shooting us." I ducked inside a vacant building and watched as my worst fears unfolded. The man was correct. Men leaned out the sides of the planes and fired at the fleeing crowds as if they were shooting cattle from the clouds. People ran about, helpless and terrified, looking for cover where ever they could find it.

The monster kept moving toward Standpipe Hill. Local guardsmen traded fire with the Greenwood men, then on to Sunset Hill where guardsmen used their standard issue thirty-caliber 1906 Springfield rifles as well as the semi-defective machine gun the police had given them.

Meanwhile, Horace Taylor, known to his friends as "Peg-leg" was putting out the word that he would not go down without a fight and for those who agreed with his stance to gather at the secret location where he had been storing weapons and ammunition. Peg-leg and others had ammunition stored behind the Paradise Baptist Church, so lone men and groups crept toward the church. The men stood in the shadows whispering until Peg-leg arrived, then he told them, "We got to protect our own. We all knew this day would come. Grab a gun and plenty of ammo and we'll stop 'em at Standpipe Hill! They will never make it into Greenwood unless they come over my dead body." The men did as he said. As quietly as they could, they slipped between buildings and shrubbery toward Standpipe Hill. They marched up the hill together, knowing all of them would not come back from the hill alive.

Several small boys followed behind them. I learned later that those boys, who were too young to fight, loaded weapons for the men on the front line during the siege. Jitneys brought ammunition, and the boys loaded and reloaded the guns to keep the men armed and able to defend themselves. The boys passed the guns to the men on the front line in a human chain and only retreated when they were overpowered by the mob advancing on them with more and better weapons, including two machine guns, one of which appeared to be fully functioning.

One of those boys was Binkley Wright, who was only ten years old at the time. He described his part in the battle and told an interviewer that the mob broke into the Mt. Zion Baptist Church because they thought ammunition and weapons were stored there, but that notion was completely false. That notion provided an excuse to burn the almost new building to the ground, that and the fact that Greenwood snipers were shooting from the bell tower of the church.

Greenwood residents were particularly proud of the newly-built Mount Zion Baptist Church. It stood at the foot of Standpipe Hill, so it was commandeered as a bastion from which to defend the town from the invading white mobs. It was a sturdy brick structure, so most thought it would be safe, but they were wrong.

The machine gun mounted on the granary had been moved with the advancing horde of invaders who used it to assault the church. White gunners began to pick off the men in the belfry and to destroy the structure with machine gun volleys. Within five or six minutes, they had opened up large gaps in the bricks, making the whole structure unstable. When the men in the church were forced to stop firing at the oncoming mob, the houses in the area almost immediately began to burn one by one, then more and more. The monster grew and advanced.

Mt. Zion Baptist Church

Then the jubilant warriors took the machine gun down, wrapped it in a canvas cover, and laid it in the bed of the truck. They rolled up the belts of ammo and empty shell casings, put them away, and drove away to re-station themselves in a more propitious location.

Chaos reigned. Greenwood residents running for their lives were halted and searched with their hands up. If the invaders did not find weapons, they searched for money. If the victims protested, they were shot. One group of women had to run through the bullets to rescue their invalid mother. They put her on a cot and ran six blocks carrying her and a bundle of clothes until they were stopped by six men who forced them to hold up their hands while they were searched for money and guns.

Civilians and police were rounding up Greenwood residents and marching them to detention areas, and even then, they were not safe. Armed groups of white men and boys as young as ten raided houses and forced residents out of their houses then lined them up on streets. One man reported asking to go back into his house to get his hat and shoes, but his answer was to be shoved into the line and marched away. After the residents were lined up, they were forced to run toward Convention Hall while their captors shot at the ground behind them. As sport would have it, they often "accidentally" aimed a bit high and hit some of the running detainees in the feet and legs. Human cruelty and sadism took over previously law-abiding citizens. Vigilantes became anonymous parts of the mob and thus emboldened.

A family on the outskirts of town was trapped in a burning house when one of them attempted to flee. The man emerged from the house to find vigilantes waiting. One of the vigilantes shot the man, and two others grabbed him and ran toward the entrance of the house with the man kicking and screaming. When they reached the open front door, they tossed the man, who was still alive, as far as they could into the flames. With one last scream, he was silent.

Farther down the same street was a small house with white shutters. It was neatly kept and had a bed of red and white petunias growing along the gravel path to the house. A neatly painted white porch swing hung from the rafters. In the back of the house was a small garden where the family grew collards and tomatoes and kept a coop full of chickens so they would have eggs for their family.

The owners had fled to safety before the mob reached the house, so the marauders ran up onto the porch and tossed a torch inside then they heard a rooster crow. Three of them ran around to the garden and threw a second torch inside the chicken coop. The chickens flew against the containing mesh trying to escape. Their screeching calls mixed with the sound of crackling and collapsing timbers in the house. One singed hen flew out through an opening burned in the roof of her enclosure. A neighbor's cow was in the garden next door. The men shot the cow and a stray pig running behind the houses. Nothing in their path would survive. The smell of death floated through the streets like a summer fog.

Perhaps the most vicious example of cruelty was inflicted on a blind and helpless man who had long been a part of the Greenwood landscape. He was not only blind, but cripple as well. Both his legs had been amputated but the stump of one was a bit longer than the other. He had a small platform with wheels that he used to scoot along the street. He had a pair of catcher's mitts on his hands which he used to propel himself. He earned his living by selling pencils and sometimes by singing Christian hymns for visitors. He was dependent on the kindness of others for survival.

He was on Main Street when the mob caught up with him. The streetcar tracks ran north and south and were laid on rough bricks on Main Street. A known outlaw and bootlegger came along in a brand new car with the top down. He and the other men in the car spied the helpless man carrying his old tin cup and scooting along the street, so they got out and tied one end of a rope to his longer stump and tied the other end to the back of a car. They took off down Main Street dragging the helpless man as fast as they could, laughing all the while. The blind beggar cried out while his head bashed against the brick pavers and the railroad tracks until he became silent. When they tired of their sport, they cut him loose and left him there.

Meanwhile on Peoria Avenue, the sound of gunfire brought Maria Morales Gutierrez out of her home to see what was going on. As she stepped out her front door, she saw two children wandering in the street alone. They had been separated from their parents in the commotion, so they were terrified. Suddenly in the sky above them, Maria heard an airplane swooping down. Men were hanging out of the plane with rifles trained on the children, but she ran to them anyway. She gathered them in her arms and hurried to the safety of her home. Later two vigilantes came to her door and demanded she give the children to them. She didn't speak much English, but she vehemently told them "No!" Somehow she convinced them to leave her and the children alone.

As the fighting wore on, small pockets of resistance remained. When guardsmen came upon these battling groups, they no longer tried to intervene to stop the fighting and looting. They made no effort to stop marauding whites, but rather joined them and participated willingly in the abuse. They either captured or killed the resistors and took what they wanted from them.

Marauders burst into one modest home where an old couple lived and demanded the man, who was 80 years old, march out of the house. The old man sat in a chair with a blanket folded over his lap because he was paralyzed. He had been talking quietly with his wife before the men burst inside. He quickly told them he could not walk, but he would go if someone would help him. His thin hands trembled as he clutched his Bible and begged the men not to hurt his wife. The men shouted at the old woman, "Get out, old woman!" One of them raised his gun toward her, and the old man looked at her through reddened eyes and told her to go. The old woman planted her feet and refused to leave her helpless husband of 65 years. She clutched the back of his chair and stood her ground, but they forced her to go anyway. While she stood on the front steps of her home begging, the men shot her husband where he sat, having never been able to move from the chair. Then they doused the old man and the floor and curtains with kerosene and torched his home. His sobbing widow was held by the mob and forced to watch as her entire life went up in flames.

Years later, George Monroe talked about hiding under his parents' bed while looters ransacked his home and took his mother away at gunpoint. Mrs. Monroe screamed as the men took her outside. She knew her children were hiding in the house, but the men didn't, and she didn't dare tell them. She tried to wrest herself free and go back in the house, but she could only watch helplessly. Five-year-old George hid with his older sisters and one older brother. They didn't make a sound, but they could see the feet of the men rifling through their parents' belongings. The men joked with each other as they searched through the bureau and cedar chest in the bedroom. When they were satisfied they had taken everything of any value, they set the curtains on fire with the children still hidden under the bed. Still the children didn't make a sound. When they were leaving, one of the men stepped on George's hand. He started to scream out in pain, but his sister slapped her hand over his mouth to stop him. The men were so preoccupied with their looting, they didn't hear the commotion under the bed, and the big boot on George's hand didn't even know it was standing on a little hand. As soon as the men left the room, the children fled out the back door to safety. The entire family lived to tell about the day, but they had no home to go back to.

As the fighting reached North Hartford, vigilantes set upon the home of Kinney Booker. The men shouted at Kinney's father, "You got a gun in here, nigger?"

Booker told them he didn't then pleaded with the mob not to burn his home. "I got nothing here. I'm not going to hurt anybody. Please don't burn my house," he begged. He had sent his wife and children, including Kinney, to the attic to hide, and he knew they would perish if the men set fire to the house.

In response to his pleas, the men sprayed the house with gasoline or possibly kerosene and set it on fire just as they had done to the old couple. Booker rushed out the front door, pretending to leave then sneaked back in when the men went on to the next house. He rescued his family from the attic, and they fled barefoot and in their night clothes to the countryside.

The Booker family left their beautifully furnished home to

burn. In it was a grand piano, which Kinney dearly loved. But Kinney's worst memory was of his sister's question as they fled. It haunted him for the rest of his life. As the frightened family fled, they could smell the smoke and see burning houses all around them. They ran with flaming telephone poles falling in their path. They dodged burning debris and stray gunfire. The children were terrified. Kinney's little sister asked him, "Kinney, is the world on fire?" He told her no, but they were in big trouble.

Not long after that, the family was captured by the local national guardsmen and taken to Convention Hall. Guardsmen appeared in front of them and snatched the children as they ran by. When their parents stopped to take their children back, all of them were captured and taken to relative safety by well-meaning guardsmen. Their time in Convention Hall was filled with terror and uncertainty since they knew their home and fortune were gone. Fortunately for the Booker children, their father worked for H.F. Wilcox, a wealthy oil man, and Wilcox came to Convention Hall and took Mrs. Booker and the children to his home. They lived in his basement for a long while. They were among the lucky ones. They had a roof over their head and food to eat even if they had a very uncertain future.

Another family that suffered insult and injury in the riot was that of Juanita Delores Burnett Arnold. Mrs. Arnold's grandparents and parents lived in Greenwood. Her grandparents owned a grocery store and a large home on Madison Street. Her father had been a teacher but left that job to work for the Oil Supply Company in the Drew Building in Tulsa. Her mother was a seamstress, who sewed for wealthy white women in Tulsa.

For this family, the problems began before the riot. Bands of angry, envious men roamed the streets and were jealous of her family's nice homes. Whites shouted racial slurs at them and encroached on her property, so her father got his gun and ordered them off. The men left, but some very reluctantly. One of the men returned the day of the riot and said, "Where is that uppity Nigger who was so bold yesterday?" Mrs. Arnold's father had left the home earlier, but if he had still been in the house, he would most certainly have been killed.

The family along with their neighbors fled when the riot started, but Mrs. Arnold's father stopped to help a man who had been shot. He told them to keep going, so they kept running until they came upon an elderly woman who couldn't keep up. They stopped to help the woman, putting themselves in danger, but that was typical of Mrs. Arnold's mother. She was kind and could not leave the woman in harm's way. She was the oldest of ten children and accustomed to taking care of others. She tried to get the children to go on ahead, but they refused.

Fortunately, Mrs. Arnold's father had asked his boss to help his family. While they were standing in the roadway frightened and confused, he came along in his car to rescue them. The man was risking his own life to save them, and he shouted for them to get in the car, but there was not room for the elderly lady they were trying to save, so they refused. The very exasperated man finally relented and took them all to safety.

The family had other good fortune that day. Mrs. Arnold's grandfather's store was saved by some white drummers who regularly called on him. They knew the family to be kind and good people, so they protected the store. The drummers arrived at the store on June 1 just as the riot began, and they did not leave until it was over. They told potential intruders that a good man owned the store, so they would not allow anyone to destroy what he had worked so hard for. They kept their word.

Even a deputy sheriff was not safe from the mob. Black Deputy Sheriff V.B. Bostic said that a white Tulsa police officer routed him and his wife from their home and set fire to it. He said they, "poured oil on the floor and set a lighted match to it." Even though he was a deputy, he had to stand helplessly by and watch his life go up in flames.

Bostic certainly never harmed anyone or participated in the

riot, but some law enforcement personnel did. One white eyewitness reported that a white police officer she knew went home and changed into plain clothes, then she saw him get into his car and go straight back to Greenwood. He led groups of whites into Greenwood homes where they pillaged at will and never once offered to protect or defend the occupants. This officer came home with his car loaded with stolen goods and unloaded it in plain sight into his home. No one seemed to think anything of this behavior, or at least if they did, they never openly criticized it. She saw him bring in furniture and a box that she assumed contained cash or jewelry. Other witnesses reported seeing this same officer kicking in doors of Greenwood homes and assisting in the destruction of those homes. His car laden with stolen goods was not the only one returning to Tulsa that day. Trucks roamed the streets hauling off everything they could carry. I saw grand pianos and other fine furnishings being towed or carried out of Greenwood. I'm told those expensive possessions showed up in white Tulsa homes for years to come, but most of the Greenwood residents never recovered from the holocaust either financially or emotionally.

Both law enforcement and guardsmen came in good and bad that day. Some, like the ones who rescued the Booker family, genuinely tried to protect terrorized Greenwood families while others participated willingly in the holocaust and plundering. Like a teacher who remembers only the two rotten students in her class, it is easy for us to remember only the evil doers, when actually many tried to stop the killing and destruction. The truth includes both—the hype only one.

Hospitals in Tulsa were filling up with injured and dead victims, but vigilantes had burned to the ground the Frissell Memorial Hospital in Greenwood before the state troops arrived and martial law could be declared. Frissell was an all-black hospital solely for use of the residents of Greenwood, so it was razed as the mobs swept through neighborhoods destroying everything in their path. That left nowhere for the Greenwood injured to go. Even if the hospital had been intact, ambulances and fire trucks were forbidden by the mob to render aid, so it would not have been much help. One young ambulance driver who tried to get into his vehicle was shot in the hand as he grabbed the door handle. Needless to say, he ran in the other direction and never got into the ambulance.

The Dreamland Theater, the elegant Stradford Hotel, the *Star* building, and Gurley's grand hotel, all were reduced to rubble. They were just burned out shells by this time. The only buildings of any value left in Greenwood were a few of the finer homes on North Detroit Avenue in an area abutting the white sections of Tulsa, but most of them would be gone also in the end.

In white Tulsa, a very different picture was unfolding. As residents began to see smoke billowing from the Greenwood sections and to hear gunfire, some cheered while others hid and some ran to join the melee. Shopkeepers were having trouble keeping their businesses open, not that they actually had many customers, but many who worked at the shops took off to join the riots.

Students at Central High School could hear the gunfire and see the smoke. Two students there bolted from class and ran to join the action. One ran past a man carrying a gun and heading back into Tulsa. The boy stopped the man and asked, "What's going on? Where's the fight?"

The man handed the brand new gun and the cartridges to the boy. He looked haggard and reeked of smoke. He told the boy, "You can have it. I'm going home and going to bed. I been up all night fightin' niggers. I'm tired. It's all out war over there, boy!"

Some merchants chose to close their businesses and join the vigilantes. Cooper's Grocer was one of those. The manager told young Guy Ashby, who worked there, "Go home, boy. There won't be no working today. I'm going hunting niggers." He took a rifle from the store and left telling Ashby to lock up. He was not alone. There seemed to be an almost festive atmosphere that day in white Tulsa. So many envious men finally had their chance to balance the sheet and they took grand pleasure in that opportunity, at least for a while.

The only bright spots in the day of destruction came from unlikely good-hearted Tulsans who helped fleeing Greenwood victims and saved some of their lives. It was these few people who kept me from losing all faith in the human race. Some were residents who had domestic servants in their homes—others were simply people who had compassion for their fellow man, regardless of color.

In more affluent neighborhoods almost all of the homes had domestic servants, and even they came under attack. Vigilantes combed those neighborhoods rounding up black servants. They demanded that maids, butlers, housekeepers, and chauffeurs be turned over to be incarcerated until the riot was quelled. For the most part, these were loyal servants who had no knowledge and certainly no part in the problems of the day. Many were turned over to the mobs but some of the home owners refused. They cared for their servants and attempted to protect them. Some who did this were attacked themselves. They were called "nigger lovers," and bricks and other objects were thrown through their windows. No one was safe in a community gone berserk. However, these domestic servants usually fared much better than their friends and relatives in Greenwood.

Mary Korte was a kind soul who worked in domestic service for a wealthy Tulsa family. She had a small farm outside Tulsa, which she turned into a make-shift refugee camp. She hid refugees at her farm for days until it was safe for them to leave. She risked her own life and property to help others.

Merrill and Ruth Phelps were a white couple who lived outside of town on the Sand Springs Road. Like Mary, they hid and fed fleeing victims for days. They helped so many of the refugees that their home became known as a "safe place." People fleeing the mobs crawled along creek beds and hid in underbrush, hungry and terrified. They passed messages among those they encountered and spread the word about safe places like the Phelps house. Others found safe harbor right under the noses of the white vandals.

A porter who worked at the YWCA building in Tulsa found refuge with Mary Jo Erhardt, a kind stenographer who lived at the YWCA. She could not sleep because of the chaos and the gunfire, so she got up early and headed downstairs, then she heard a voice she recognized. The porter was at the door begging, "Miss Mary! Oh, Miss Mary! Let me in quick."

Armed men were chasing him. Mary Jo quickly opened the door and snatched him inside. The only place she could think of to hide him was the walk-in freezer. She told him, "Quick, get in the freezer!" She opened up the walk-in freezer in the large kitchen area and shoved him inside. Just as she closed the freezer door and got him hidden, three men started banging on the door, which fortunately was securely locked. Three vigilantes stood peering in at her, each with a revolver pointed at her.

Mary Jo barked, "What do you want?" at the men. She recalled years later that, although she should have been afraid of the men, she was not. She said she had never felt hatred before in her life, but she hated these men.

The men shouted, "Where did he go?"

Mary Jo answered with disgust, "Where did *who* go?"

"That nigger," one of them replied. "Did you let him in?"

Mary Jo honestly answered, "Mister, I'm not letting *anybody* in here!" In her mind that was honest because she definitely had already let in all the people she intended to let in.

Mary Jo waited 10 minutes until she felt safe to let the porter out. By that time, the man, who was clad in thin clothing since it was quite hot outside, was nearly frozen, but he lived to tell about the day.

Clara Kimble, a white teacher at Central High School was

another compassionate soul that day. She opened up her home to her counterparts at Booker T. Washington High School as did others. Some donated food, clothing, money and other forms of assistance. This was a human disaster unlike anything these people could have imagined, and all struggled to make sense of it and to cope with the aftermath. Many hung their heads in shame and hid their secrets for the rest of their lives.

Finally, the state National Guard units arrived at the depot around 9:15 am on June 1. They were a group of 109 soldiers and officers. According to most witnesses, they did their job as they should. Not one of them was ever accused of adding to the destruction, unlike their local counterparts. They were all white, in uniform, and well armed, but they used that power to stop both black and white marauders. They were there to protect Oklahomans regardless of color. Unfortunately, they were too late to prevent most of the destruction, and some say they took time to have a nice breakfast before they started into the riot-torn town. After considerable efforts to abide by legal protocol, martial law was declared at 11:30 am, and the state troops began to round up straggling bands of black Tulsans and herd them to safety. Others rounded up and disarmed white vigilantes still intent on destroying Greenwood and its residents.

Brigadier General Charles F. Barrett later said that he had never seen such scenes as he witnessed that day. He reported that all the Greenwood section seemed to be on fire and 25,000 whites, armed to the teeth were roaming the area in ruthless defiance of law and order. He watched as motorcars roamed the city firing at will at innocent by-standers. His personal account of what he saw supports claims by Greenwood residents of unspeakable abuse.

While the necessary protocol for declaring martial law was being met, some of the most valuable homes in Greenwood were under siege. These homes were located along North Detroit Avenue and A. J. Smitherman's fine home where I had enjoyed dinner was one of them. Booker T. Washington High School's principal, Ellis W. Woods also lived there as did Thomas R. Gentry and Dr. Bridgewater. Since this was an area on the fringes of Greenwood, it had escaped harm, but that would not last.

John A. Oliphant, a white attorney who lived nearby, had been calling police headquarters all morning trying to get protection for these residences. The homes had already been looted, but they had not been burned, so he was desperately trying to keep that from happening. He felt certain that if ten officers were sent over there, they would be able to protect the homes. He also asked the fire department to come, all to no avail. The fire department had been forbidden to come into Greenwood to put out the fires or to prevent them. He pleaded that millions of dollars worth of real estate could still be saved. His pleas fell on the wrong ears. Getting no help from the police, Oliphant was encouraged when he saw the state troops had arrived, so he asked for fifteen or twenty of them to be sent to North Detroit.

Before the guardsmen could be dispatched, a group of "special deputies" became aware of the fact that these homes had not been destroyed, so they immediately headed for North Detroit. They arrived around 10:30 am just before martial law was declared. There were only three or four of them, and all were wearing badges. Instead of protecting these elegant homes, they immediately set fire to them. The state troops finally came, but they were too late. Only Dr. Bridgewater's home was saved, but it been looted.

Bridgewater considered himself lucky, but he lost most of his assets. He had been away at a medical conference. When he returned home, he was held at the Convention Hall with other Greenwood residents. When he was finally released and allowed to return to his home, he was sickened. All his elegant furniture was piled in the street, his safe had been broken open and all of the money stolen, all his silverware was gone, his family Bible was gone, his electric light fixtures were broken, his widow lights were broken as well as all the glass in his doors, his dishes were all either stolen or broken, his floors were covered with broken glass, and his phone was torn from the wall. Still, he was grateful he had a home. He was one of very few residents in Greenwood who still had a roof over his head.

While Dr. Bridgewater's home was being looted, a final skirmish was taking place near the Santa Fe railroad tracks just off Peoria Avenue. Greenwood defenders had held off white marauders until noon by gathering at the railroad embankment, but a second group of whites approached with high-powered rifles. The Greenwood men were overrun, and the fighting finally ceased.

Mobs have a mentality all their own. Men who might have been benevolent bystanders before Memorial Day assumed another mien entirely. Most of the vigilantes had begun to tire by the time the state troops arrived, so they went home to count their booty and to rest. Others continued to fight and loot.

Greenwood residents had fled in all directions. It would be months before all of them were located. They began to evaluate their status, having lost all that was dear to them and all they had worked so hard to accumulate. Some would rebuild, but even that was made nearly impossible by laws enacted to deter them. White Tulsa did not want them, but many had no place else to go.

Sheriff McCullough slipped out of Tulsa without notice, taking Dick Rowland, who was later exonerated of any crime, with him. Sarah Page refused to prosecute and eventually moved away never to return to Tulsa and the day of the holocaust.

During this time of distress and recovery, many individuals and organizations stepped up to help. Among those was the Red Cross. They provided services for the refugees and assisted as much as resources would allow. Also many local churches assisted all who were in need regardless of color or creed. In addition to these charitable organizations, one family stood out. The Zarrow family reached out and assisted many of the Greenwood residents and gave unselfishly of their time and resources.

The Holocaust

The rubble of Greenwood after June 1, 1921

The Fight for Standpipe Hill

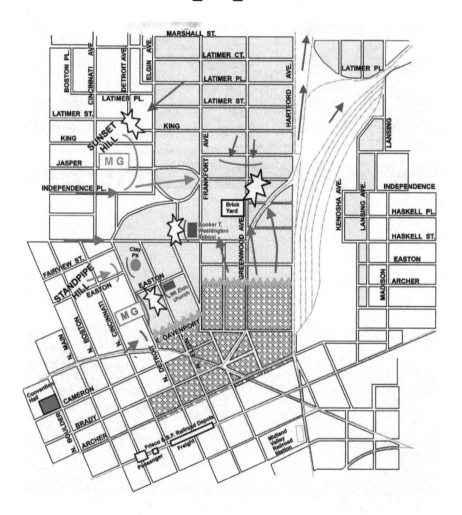

Martial Law and the Final Fight

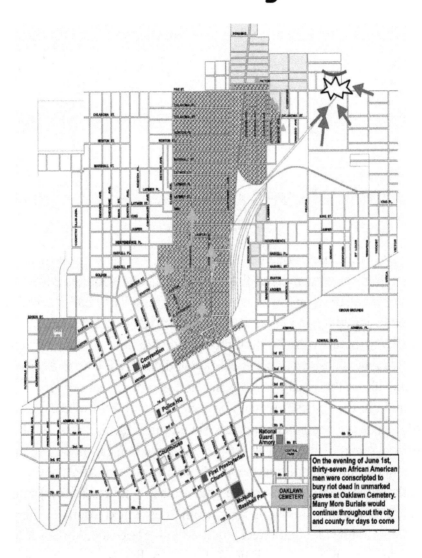

On the evening of June 1st, thirty-seven African American men were conscripted to bury riot dead in unmarked graves at Oaklawn Cemetery. Many More Burials would continue throughout the city and county for days to come

CHAPTER 9

THE AFTERMATH

When the smoke began to clear and the state troops had control of the city, most of the remaining Greenwood residents were corralled in one of several holding areas. They had ostensibly been rounded up and taken in for "protective custody" when in reality, officials were holding them to ensure none of them stirred up trouble. These were often women and children, who had been going about their business in peace and had never caused any trouble in their lives. I walked past the baseball field where many of them were being held and saw blank faces, faces struck dumb by terror and disbelief. These were teachers, nurses, shop keepers, mothers, fathers, children, people from all walks of life. They gathered in small groups, some with arms around each other, some sobbing, but none knowing what would come next. Many of them were still unaware that Greenwood no longer existed. Some sat on the dusty ground with their heads buried in their hands. Many were barefooted and some still wearing nightshirts. All were sitting in the blistering sun, and few had any shelter from the heat. None cared.

I stood for a long while watching them in this slow motion image of sorrow and desolation. I recognized no one, but some were surely people I had met, perhaps the piano player at Gurley's or Johnson, Smitherman's butler. All had been changed so dramatically in one twenty-four hour glitch in human history that they were rendered unrecognizable forever. My gut ached, and I became ill. I walked to the side of the road and held on to a street sign to steady myself. When I was able, I walked toward Greenwood. I was white, so I was free, or was I? Are any of us ever free? Confusion paralyzed most of us that day.

As I walked toward Greenwood, I passed a row of houses, mostly small and in relative disrepair. Outside one of them was a group of men laughing and hauling things out of the bed of a truck.

The first man shouted, "Hey Jack, help me with this here thing. Ain't she a beaut?"

The man was attempting to remove a finely carved mahogany dresser from his truck. His buddy replied, "Hell yeah! Reckon it's got any money in them fancy drawers?" They both laughed and snatched the drawers loose, searching each one. They found a little girl's hairbrush with a sterling silver handle and a matching mirror.

"Look here, Jack! This here thing must be worth a fortune. This is genuine silver. Reckon how much we can get for it? Some of them fancy folks sure gonna pay a pretty penny for it."

I hurried on down the street before they started unloading the rest, but I saw evidence all along the way of stolen goods taken from Greenwood, so much of it that thousands of dollars worth of personal belongings sat blistering in the hot Oklahoma sun waiting to be transported or brought inside ram-shackle houses.

But the looting and hooting of that neighborhood did not prepared me for what I saw next. What I saw reminded me of a war poem written by Isaac Rosenberg. Some refer to it as "Dead Man's Dump." It describes carts carrying war dead to the dump to be disposed of. They hung off carts and stuck out like crowns of thorns. These men, who had yesterday been fathers, brothers, and husbands protecting their own, were now rotting in the sun and sticking out like crowns of thorns.

Anyone with a pickup truck was conscripted to haul bodies to the cemetery like the men pushing the carts in "Dead Man's Dump." Others had been ordered to bury the dead as quickly as possible in unmarked and un-grieved holes in the ground. Two sweating men slung dirt from a cavern in the earth until they declared it sufficient to hold a body then one of them shouted, "Bring one on over here, boys. This will do."

Two young men with stone faces grabbed a body from the pile, one grappling with the arms—the other struggling to carry the feet. They laid it as carefully as they could into the hole. The boys brushed their hands together as if to banish the stench and dirt. One took a soiled handkerchief from his pocket and wiped sweat from his neck. Both looked away toward town. Neither spoke. Neither was old enough to have graduated from high school

No casket, no marker, no family, no final words, the bodies were just gone. The men began to shovel dirt over the slumped body as the two boys made their way back over to the stack of bodies to wait for the next request for a body to be cast into an opening in the earth. The men had been told to get the bodies in the ground as quickly as possible and never to talk about it. Crates of bodies sat around waiting for their final resting place. This went on for several days, while the families of the dead waited in groups detained by state troops or local authorities. Many never learned the fate of their loved ones. They were never able to grieve beside a grave or say a prayer over a loved one's body.

I walked by one of the trucks waiting for the grave diggers and saw a young boy atop the heap. His face showed abject terror as if he had literally been frightened to death. Beside him was an old man with tufts of white hair above each ear. He must have been 80 years old. He had half of his skull blown away and clotted blood covered much of his face. The heat made the bodies decay quickly. I took my handkerchief from my pocket and held it over my nose.

I suppose these men in the shallow holes in the ground were better off than some. Rumor suggests that upwards of 120 men and boys were buried in these shallow graves. Many others were unceremoniously tossed into the Arkansas River, disposed of quickly and cleanly without a trace. No one knows how many died, how they died, or even who they were.

I continued trudging on towards Greenwood, lost in my thoughts and struggling to understand how all this happened.

I started up Archer and turned onto North Elgin. Soon I could see the burned shell of the new Mt. Zion Baptist Church. The people of Greenwood had put their hearts and souls into building this new place of worship. It had been dedicated only a couple of months earlier, but now it was blackened rubble. Bricks from the handsome bell tower lay all around. A small dog sniffed the still smoldering embers of something that was once a pew. Part of the fur on the dog's tail was singed, and he had smut across his face. I wandered from street to street sickened by what I saw.

Gone was the Dreamland Theater. Its sign drooped, refusing to give up and fall to the street, but its glory was no more. Doc's Beanery, Hamburger Kelly's café, Mable Little's beauty salon, Rolly and Ada Huff's Confectionery on Archer where you could get a killer sarsaparilla or even a cold soda, gone. Gurley's fine hotel where I had drunk the sterling lemonade and listened to the fine piano player, gone. Smitherman's *Tulsa Star*, gone. Then I reached Smitherman's fine home where I had been shown such grand hospitality, gone, just ashes, gutted and looted. But the saddest spot of all was when I came to Dr. Jackson's home. Blood still stained the earth where he fell. The house was a heap of charred sticks and bricks, but the blood on the earth was the worst of it. I had already heard what happened to him. He was a gentle soul who sought nothing more than to be of service to his fellow man, to relieve suffering where ever he could. He was 40 years old—with so many years of service left in him. I left Greenwood that day a different man from the one who boarded a train in New York and headed west to seek fame and fortune.

When the authorities finally released most of the Greenwood residents, they wandered for days trying to find loved ones and the few possessions they had left. Most were penniless and had nowhere to go. Charity groups and a few local citizens tried to help, but the survivors scattered to the four winds, destroyed by Memorial Day. I talked to many of them in the hopeless days that followed and kept their stories close to my heart all these years. This is their story, not mine.

I could not bear to remain in Oklahoma and be reminded each day of this jagged rip in the fabric of humanity, so I once again boarded a train and let fate take me where it would. That's how I wound up shoveling manure instead of human garbage.

I learned later that more than a dozen of the Greenwood men were charged with the riot, but not a single white person was ever charged. J.B. Stradford had to flee, jumping bail his son posted for him. Some were insistent on hanging him for his role in the riot. He spent the rest of his life trying to clear his name, but not until 1996 was he finally cleared of any wrong doing. He had died more than 60 earlier. He lost everything he had and was never able to return to Oklahoma. He established a successful practice in Chicago, but he was a broken man for the rest of his life. He was guilty only of trying to reason with men who had no reason in them and of being a grand example of the American Dream come true, a dream that ended in a nightmare three years to the day after his fine hotel first opened its doors.

The disaster did not end with the riot. Only six days after the riot, Tulsa City Commission passed ordinances that made it virtually impossible for Greenwood to rebuild. The ordinances were declared unconstitutional and overturned, so some Greenwood residents did rebuild eventually, but many were forced to spend the winter of 1921-22 living in tents and others left the area forever.

What an irony that all this destruction occurred on Memorial Day, a day first set aside to celebrate veterans of the American Civil War, a war to free African Americans and give them a better life. An irony, indeed.

Picking up the pieces of ruined lives

CHAPTER 10

GREENWOOD PROFILES

O.W. Gurley was the founding father of Greenwood. Without him there would have been no Greenwood. As a young  man, he earned a presidential appointment from President Grover Cleveland, an appointment which he resigned to follow his dream in the West. He acquired land in the Oklahoma Land run of 1889, but he later sold that land and purchased forty acres in what was to become Greenwood. He saw the investment potential there and parlayed his investment into what amounted at that time to an empire. He started with one rooming house to accommodate African Americans, who were arriving by the hundreds in Tulsa to seek employment and freedom from post-war prejudice. Ironically the prejudice they were trying to escape later destroyed Greenwood and most of the wealth accumulated there. Gurley's largest investment in Greenwood was his hotel on Greenwood Avenue. It was a landmark and was completely razed along with all Gurley's other investments and properties. He survived the riot and disappeared. He was charged along with many of his associates with inciting the riot, but he was never prosecuted since he could not be found. His associate, B.C. Franklin, noted in his memoirs that Gurley had gone to California. Rumors circulated in Tulsa that Gurley had been killed in the riot, but that appears not to have been true.

J.B. Stradford was the son of a freed Kentucky slave born

in 1861. He graduated from Oberlin College and Indiana Law School. In 1899 he moved his wife, Augusta, and their children to Tulsa. He became the wealthiest African American in Tulsa. His monetary loses in the Tulsa riot are said to have exceeded $200,000, a considerable sum in 1921, but it was not the monetary losses that troubled him most. His good name was ruined, and he was powerless to defend himself. Officials in Tulsa charged him with inciting the riot and his son, also a lawyer, posted bail. Stradford jumped bail and left Oklahoma forever. He and his family moved to Chicago after the riot where he enjoyed a successful law practice, but the charges leveled against him haunted him until his death in 1935. Those charges were not dropped until 1996. Family members have stated that Stradford was only trying to act as a peacemaker when he went to the courthouse to try to talk to the men who were gathering there to protect Dick Rowland. He died an angry, depressed man because of these false charges.

W.D. Williams and his family owned and operated the Dreamland Theater as well as rental houses, a garage, a confectionary store, and rooming houses. They were the first Greenwood family to own a car. Always an entrepreneur, when he bought the car, Williams learned how to repair it, so it seemed natural for him to open a business to do this for other owners who came later. The family lost everything in the riot. When the riot started, Williams stood on top of the theater and shot at intruders who were trying to take his possessions, but that was not to last. He was far outnumbered. He managed to survive, and his resourceful wife had somehow managed to keep some of her money, so they rebuilt most of their holdings, but the property that had been the Dreamland Theater was sold to make way for an expressway through the area. The city of Tulsa passed ordinances immediately after the riot making it extremely difficult to rebuild. These ordinances were later struck down, and those who could, began a limited recovery.

Dr. R.T. Bridgewater was a well-liked physician in Greenwood. He had been the leader of an attempt in 1919 to ensure the safety of two young men who had been arrested in Tulsa. He led a group of men to the jail and spoke with the sheriff. That encounter was defused, so Bridgewater and his group returned peacefully to Greenwood. When the 1921 riot began, Bridgewater was out of town at a medical conference and was detained at Convention Hall when he returned. When he was finally allowed to return to his home to collect his medical bag, he found that his home had been ransacked but that the home itself was still standing. He considered himself fortunate that he still had a home, but he was sorely distressed by the condition of that home. When he saw his home, Bridgewater said,

> On reaching the house, I saw my piano and all of my elegant furniture piled in the street. My safe had been broken open, all of the money stolen, also my silverware,

cut glass, all of the family clothes, and everything of value had been removed, even my family Bible. My electric light fixtures were broken, all of the window lights and glass in the doors were broken, the dishes that were not stolen were broken, the floors were covered (literally speaking) with glass, even the phone was torn from the wall. (Tulsa Reparations Committee Report)

B.C. Franklin was a relative new comer to Tulsa when the riot occurred. He was a lawyer with Native American roots in Oklahoma but he attended college in Tennessee and Georgia. He opened a law practice in Rentiesville, Oklahoma, and also served as postmaster, justice of the peace, and businessman, but those jobs did not pay well, so he abandoned that to set up a law practice in Greenwood in February 1921, just three months before the riot. He quickly became friends with many influential men in Greenwood and survived the riot. He later wrote his memoirs, which included information about the riot and his friends.

Dick Rowland and Sarah Page were both orphans and both disappeared into obscurity after the riot. Sarah issued a written statement refusing to press charges against Rowland, so the law had no choice but to release him. Some say Rowland went to Kansas City. Others have hinted that Page went there also, but no reliable records exit on either of them after the riot. A few people who knew them say they were "courting," but other who also knew them say that they are sure that didn't happen since Rowland was such a shy boy and would never have approached a white woman. Comments have been made as to Page's reputation and have hinted that she may have earned money for sexual favors, but those are mere speculations. No proof of any such behavior is noted. Some questioned how she earned enough money to support herself although she was an employee of the Drexel Building while she was attending secretarial school. It is reasonable to assume, however, that they knew each other since they worked in close proximity to each other and would have most certainly had contact when Rowland used the elevator Page operated.

Binkley Wright was only ten years old when the riot occurred, so he was not involved in the shooting, but he played an important role in helping those who were doing the shooting. Wright and his friends often stole rides into Tulsa on the jitneys that transported passengers back and forth to town. The boys would grab onto the spare tire on the side of the vehicle and hang on until it got where ever they wanted to go. They were in town when the problems began. When they heard of the trouble, they hopped another jitney and got back to Greenwood, where they were conscripted by a group led by Peg-leg Taylor. The boys hacked open crates of ammunition and loaded weapons for the men defending Greenwood. They handed the loaded guns up the line in a human chain until the men were picked off by the vigilantes with machine guns. Wright survived, but his family lost everything they owned. The saddest part for him was that the family lost all its photographs. He knew they could never be replaced. After the riot, Wright's parents divorced, and he moved to California with his mother.

Kinney Booker was a small boy living on North Hartford when the riot occurred. The family lived in a lovely, elegantly furnished home. Those furnishing included a grand piano, which was lost along with everything the family owned during the riot. The family barely escaped the holocaust, barefoot and in their night clothes. Kinney's father, a very resourceful man, worked for a Tulsa oil man named Wilcox, so after the riot, Booker was able to rebuild a home for his family, but it was never as grand as the one they lost. They never again had a grand piano.

John Melvin Alexander had an interesting story to tell about the day of the riot although he was only three years old at the time. His family lived on North Norfolk, and his house survived while all of his neighbors' houses were burned to the ground. He said his father left their home open when they fled up Pine Street and were picked up by the National Guard and taken to the ball park on Eleventh Street. He had no guns in the house, and he said the Lord told him to leave the house unlocked. When the vigilantes came to his house, they looked through it and saw no guns, so they left it virtually untouched. After the riot, his was the only house standing in the area, so he took in as many friends and neighbors as could fit in the house and housed and fed them as long as he could. Alexander later fought in the Coral Sea in WW II.

Clarence Fields added interesting insights into the melee when he was interviewed by the Tulsa Reparations Committee. He was part of the riot, being both shot at and shooting back at the invaders. Men in one of the airplanes shot at him and wounded him slightly after which he returned fire. It was his broad outlook in hindsight that gave extra insight, however. He stated that his family had come to Oklahoma with the Native Americans in the Trail of Tears march. He indicated that many African-Americans intermarried with Native Americans, and that practice riled some white Oklahomans. He also said some factions in Oklahoma sought to prevent intermarriage between Native and African American citizens to prevent African Americans from acquiring land through Indian land allotments. He believes many oil barons got their oil-rich land by marrying into those same land allotments.

Dr. A.C. Jackson was a nationally recognized surgeon who was said by the Mayo Clinic to be the best African-American surgeon in the country. Jackson was one of fifteen African-American physicians in Tulsa at the time of the riot. He was only forty years old when he was gunned down outside his Greenwood home as he stood facing the vigilantes with his hands up. He told the mob that he was unarmed and that he wanted to go with them. He believed they were there to

Yours Fraternally,
Dr. A. C. Jackson,
Consulting Physician & Surgeon
Chronic diseases and diseases of Women a Specialty.
Calls made in the country.   Phone 2573   In office at Night.
Corner Greenwood and Archer   Tulsa, Okla.

take him to safety at Convention Hall. As he walked out onto his front lawn, two men shot him down. While he was lying on the lawn, another man shot him in the leg. He bled to death in tremendous pain, unable to get help from the medical profession he so loved. He was a gentle man who sought only to do good for humanity and was beloved by both black and white associates.

Dr. Olivia J. Hooker was one of the most endearing of the survivors of this tragic event. Born on February 12, 1915, she was just six years old when the riot occurred, but she has vivid memories and talks about them openly. She was apparently the last survivor of this event. At the age of 102, her mind was as sharp as ever when she was interviewed. She later passed away on November 21, 2018. She received a Bachelor of Arts from Ohio State University in 1937, a Master's in 1947 from Teachers College of Columbia University, and a Ph.D. from the University of Rochester in 1961. She was the first woman to serve in the US Coast Guard, earning the rank of Yeoman, Second Class. After World War II was over, she worked with women with severe learning disabilities and was able to teach many of them things they were said to be incapable of learning because she approached them with an open mind and refused to believe they couldn't learn. After that, she taught at Fordham University until her retirement in 1985. Never daunted by anything, she joined the Coast Guard Auxiliary at the age of 95. She is representative of the spirit that built Greenwood. Only a community with exceptional strength and ability could have created such a community, and this spirit followed them as they were chased from their homes. Like Smitherman and many of the other survivors, nothing could stop her from excelling, but never again were all these extraordinary people grouped into one single town. She was instrumental in establishing the Tulsa Race Riot Commission, demanding reparations for herself and other survivors of the Memorial Day massacre. A celebration of her success and her amazing personality can be found on Facebook as her many fans celebrate her life (https://www.facebook.com/dr.oliviahookerfanpage/).

Andrew J. Smitherman was arguably the most significant figure in this tragedy. He had his finger on the pulse of Greenwood and the country. He was educated, intelligent, and passionate about his cause. He was born in Childersburg, Alabama, in 1883. His family moved to Indian Territory in the 1890's. He attended the University of Kansas and Northwestern University as well as LaSalle University in Philadelphia, where he earned a law degree. He married Ollie Murphy in 1910, and they had five children. Always active in Civil Rights issues, Smitherman was instrumental in bringing justice after a white mob burned more than 20 homes in Dewey, Oklahoma, in 1917. This involvement brought him to the attention of the Governor of Oklahoma, who invited Smitherman to serve on a committee for racial justice.

He began his publishing career in Muskogee, Oklahoma, and later moved to Tulsa to found the *Daily Tulsa Star*. His articles in the *Star* encouraged Greenwood residents to protect their own with deadly force if necessary. When the riot occurred, Smitherman lost everything he owned but was able to get out of Tulsa along with his family. The family went to Massachusetts and later settled in Buffalo where he resumed his journalistic pursuits. Like Bridgewater, Smitherman was blamed for the riot, but extradition efforts failed, so he was never brought back to Oklahoma to stand trial. He died in 1961 in Buffalo, New York.

As a result of the riot, the KKK moved into Tulsa with vengeance. Smitherman's nephew, a deputy sheriff in Tulsa, was attacked a year after the riot by the KKK, who cut off part of his ear as a show of force.

After escaping the Memorial Day massacre, Smitherman wrote "Eulogy to the Tulsa Martyrs," a poem expressing his feelings of pride and regret. He published this poem along with several others in a four-page book, which is now among those held in the Rare Books Repository at Beinecke Library at Yale University.

Eulogy to the Tulsa Martyrs

If I could stand in the midst of the dead bodies
Of those brave black men who fell in the Tulsa riot and massacre,
As martyrs to the greatest cause it has ever been human privilege
> *to espouse,*
I would lift my eyes in adoration and gratitude
To the great God of the universe who gave us their being
And my voice to their fellowmen throughout this broad land,
And on behalf of a grateful race pay homage to their blessed
> *memory.*
By way of eulogy it may well be said, that
Because of them, the hope of our race looms brighter
And the world has been made some better;
Not because they lived in it, but because they died as they did
True martyrs to a sacred cause!
Fighting against overwhelming odds, and without hope of
> *surviving the conflict,*
These men gave their all that a great principle might triumph.
Tis better to fight, and die if need be,

Than to live, if to live means to compromise manhood
And to sacrifice the sacred things that life is made of.
There is no choice for the man who is a man,
No matter what the realms of life may hold,
Nor how sweet the unveiled future may appear,
But to fight when contumelie is the sting, And in fighting die, if
*   perchance he cannot win.*
Tis to the honor and glory of any man
To give his all for the things he holds dear.
Sleep! Sleep on, my fallen comrades,
Rest complacently in the joy that must come to you,
Even beyond the veil of death,
In the consciousness that you have contributed a full measure
To the cause of human justice,
Your active beings we have no more—
These, and all that in them was,
You freely gave on the altar of human sacrifice
But your spirits abide yet with us
A glorious inspiration to twelve million kindred souls
And their posterity to unborn generations
Who shall ever cherish your memory
And emulate the noble example you have left us.
Sleep! Sleep on, brave souls, And may God give peace to your
*   ashes.*

Smitherman continued to fight for the rights of all men as long as he lived. As a charter member of the NAACP, he encouraged others to continue the fight. In another of his poems, he speaks of winning a great victory in Tulsa. He includes these profound lines in a letter written in January of 1922 addressed to Walter White, Assistant Secretary of the NAACP. The final stanza of the poem gives us direction in our ongoing struggle for equality and respect for our fellow human beings:

But such crimes against the Negro
In these proud United States

Meet the plaudits of the masses
Even burnings at the stakes.
Tulsa with the teeming millions
Paid the toll for racial strife,
But the black men won a victory
With their blood they paid the price.
Nobly they had stopped a lynching,
Taught a lesson for all time,
Saved a man the Court has since found
Innocent of any crime.
Though they fought the sacrificial
Fight, with banners flying high,
Yet the thing of more importance
Is the way they fought—and why!

Indeed, it was the way they fought and why! Smitherman throughout his life sought racial freedom and respect for all. A devout Roman Catholic, he believed the struggle could be won. He said:

Justice for All
No fame I ask, nor honor seek;
No empty words of praise;
My work is with the low and meek
Their state and mine to raise.
I ask no special favors;
Nor seek for mine the best;
I simply plead for justice for
My own with all the rest.
What right have you to curtail me?
Or I to hinder you?
A right that's good for one should be
For all, not a few.
My faults are yours and yours are mine:

And with each all must bear:
God in His wisdom draws his line,
His love alike we share.
No matter what good fortune, or
Ill-fortune may befall,
Tis yours and mine to share it for
We're brothers, one and all.

Considering his fervor and genuine desire to make race relations better, it is a sad testimony to our country that this tragedy remained hidden from the public for nearly a century. Smitherman did all he could, but he was a man of color in a black and white world. His voice was silenced for too many years, but today his words ring loud and clear. He will be heard at last.

EPILOG

Many have questioned my motives for writing this account of the 1921 Greenwood Riot, and I have questioned them myself, but I finally came to the conclusion that I had to write it. As a mother, a student, a teacher, a writer, and as a woman, I've always believed that the more we understand about our fellow human beings, the better we can get along. I have tried to foster understanding with these words. We can only understand if we tell the truth openly. Only the truth will protect us from future disaster. If we remain silent, we will be neither free nor safe.

If we take the time to get to know people around us, we can make better choices and live more fully. We are all one race, the human race. We are all different, but we are all the same. I once taught a class at Florida State University in which I had students from eleven different countries. That was probably the most difficult teaching assignment I have ever had, but it was undoubtedly my most rewarding teaching moment. Some of them were highly skilled in speaking and writing English, but some could barely put a subject and verb together in English although they were quite proficient in their native tongue. Those students taught me far more than I taught them. A beautiful girl from Ghana, who spoke and wrote perfect British English, tutored a sweetheart from China, who was a science whiz and proficient in Chinese but could barely write a complete sentence in English. They became quite close during the semester. Each gained a new understanding of academic strengths and weaknesses, but more importantly, of different cultures. And Danny from Venezuela, he was the class charmer and a world-class swimmer. He brightened the class with his smile, and a fellow swimmer from Canada helped him with his English language skills. I paired the students according to strengths and weaknesses and watched as students taught students, and all of them grew. By the end of the semester, most of them were reasonably proficient in writing, but all of us had become members of the world community. All of us learned that people are the same regardless of where they live, what color they are, or which language they speak.

We all love, cry, hurt, learn, celebrate, and yes, sometimes hate, but the more we know about our fellow man, the less likely we are to focus on hate. We do more loving and celebrating than hating when we see our fellow man as just that. If this story opens the eyes of only a few, my efforts will have been worthwhile. People are not colors or religions or Americans or Africans—they are people. Each one has a past. That past may include injustice, injury, loneliness, loss, and regret, and that past *will* influence actions. Faulkner insisted that "the past is not dead. In fact, it's not even past." It never is. It makes us who we are.

Sam Stackhouse is a fictional character not intended to represent any actual person, but his voice is a way of seeing events in retrospect. The rest of the characters and the story are all depicted as nearly as possible to reality. All events are factual according to historical accounts. Hindsight is always 20/20, but no one in Tulsa had the advantage of hindsight in 1921. We do, however. We don't have to let events such as this occur ever again.

I often consider Thomas Wolfe's words and his perspective on the ways in which past events guide our present actions. Sometimes we are aware of the events that shape us, but often we are not. Wolfe saw clearly how events of the past determine the present. In *Look Homeward Angel*, Wolfe wrote:

"Each of us is all the sums he has not counted: subtract us into nakedness and night again, and you shall see begin in Crete four thousand years ago the love that ended yesterday in Texas. The seeds of our destruction will blossom in the desert, the alexin of our cure grows by a mountain rock, and our lives are haunted by a Georgia slattern, because a London cut-purse went unhung. Each moment is the fruit of forty thousand years. The minute-winning days, like flies, buzz home to death, and every moment is a window on all time."

If Roy Belton had not been lynched.......If the *Tribune* had not condoned lynching as a way of deterring crime.....If the *Tribune* had not suggested a lynching when Dick Rowland was accused.....If so many prisoners had not escaped from the jail in May, 1921.....If the *Tribune* had not published the inflammatory editorial.....If Smitherman had not been insistent on Greenwood men arming themselves to protect their own.....If the crime wave in Tulsa had been handled differently.....If Dick Rowland had not worked on Memorial Day......If Sarah Page had not worked that day......If the State National Guard had arrived sooner.....If oil had not been discovered in Oklahoma.....If Jim Crow laws had not forced Greenwood to exist......If O.W. Gurlely had not bought land in Tulsa.....If.....

But all these things did happen. We can't change any of them, but we can move toward a better future where these things don't have to happen again. Langston Hughes understood this better than most. He was writing poetry during the same era that this story took place, but his words, like all great literature are universal and eternal. They apply today, perhaps more than ever. We would all be better off if we listened and took to heart his poem about a mother telling a son how to live. Hughes wrote:

Well, son, I'll tell you:
Life for me ain't been no crystal stair.
It's had tacks in it,
And splinters,
And boards torn up,
And places with no carpet on the floor—

Bare.
But all the time
I'se been a-climbin' on,
And reachin' landin's,
And turnin' corners,
And sometimes goin' in the dark
Where there ain't been no light.
So boy, don't you turn back.
Don't you set down on the steps
'Cause you finds it's kinder hard.
Don't you fall now—
For I'se still goin', honey,
I'se still climbin',
And life for me ain't been no crystal stair.

There were no crystal stairs for anyone living in Tulsa in 1921, but those who keep climbing and turning corners will survive regardless of the past. They will be protected by the truth, not destroyed by the hype.

OTHER BOOKS BY THIS AUTHOR

Behind the Tupelo Tree

A Civil War

The Ghost of Blackwater Creek

Illusions of Honor: The Truth and the Myth

Shooter Giggers

Fins and Friends: 70 Years of Diving and Spearfishing

Eminent Danger

B'ar Yarns: Florida Pioneer Stories

The Magic Dolphin

Salem's Theocracy: Shattered on the Rock of Witchcraft

Finding Ann: The Silent Journey

Thomas Wolfe: Aline Bernstein's Dark Brooding Flower

Blue Butterfly Days: Dreams and Regrets